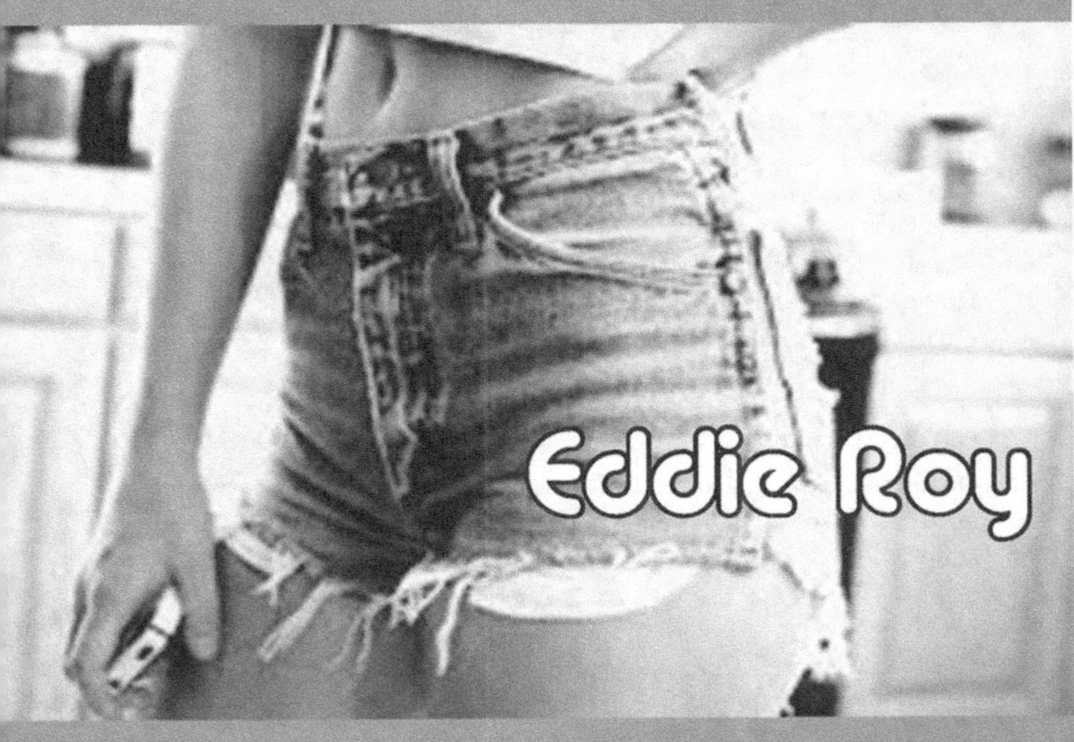

COMFORTABLE SHORTS

Eddie Roy

a dozen short easy reads

This publication contains the opinions and ideas of its author. It is intended to provide helpful and informative material on the subjects addressed in the publication. The author and publisher specifically disclaim all responsibility for any liability, loss or risk, personal or otherwise, which is incurred as a consequence, directly or indirectly, of the use and application of any of the contents of this book.

WORKBOOK PRESS LLC
187 E Warm Springs Rd,
Suite B285, Las Vegas, NV 89119, USA

Website: https://workbookpress.com/
Hotline: 1-888-818-4856
Email: admin@workbookpress.com

Ordering Information:
Quantity sales. Special discounts are available on quantity purchases by corporations, associations, and others. For details, contact the publisher at the address above.

Library of Congress Control Number:
ISBN-13:   978-1-958176-54-2 (Paperback Version)
                978-1-958176-55-9 (Digital Version)

REV. DATE: 06/02/2022

Comfortable Shorts

A dozen short easy reads

Eddie Roy

Preface:

Writing a book can be hard work; especially writing a novel. I know, at this point I've written four of them.

That doesn't mean there's no satisfaction in doing it, like there's satisfaction in doing any of a thousand other difficult things. And writing short stories can be hard work, too, but writing these stories wasn't. They came to me over a period of time, sometimes singly, sometimes in a group. The oldest story here is at least fifteen years old. The newest, six months. What they have in common is that none of them were hard work, they all are basically pretty positive and they were enjoyable to write. I hope they're enjoyable to read.

TABLE OF CONTENTS

S WESTERN SUITE

SADDLE TRAMP

The man leaning against the bar had the unmistakable look of a gunslinger. It showed in his relaxed stance; elbow on the bar top, and the heel of one polished boot hooked over the brass bar-rail. It also showed in the supremely confident smirk he wore. His whole body was relaxed save for the hand hovering over his gun.

The boy across the saloon was his polar-opposite. No more than sixteen, and too inexperienced even to know how to properly strap on a gun; he was terrified. The belt hung too low, the weight of the gun in the holster drawing it lopsided across his waist, giving him the look of a child playing dress-up in his father's clothes; which he may have been. The tie-down at the bottom of the holster was slack around his leg. His chances of dying were extremely high, and he knew it. The odor of his fear spread through the saloon as the stain of it spread down his leg. The men scattered in the dark corners of the hot, gloomy room wanted to laugh at the kid, but knew that the slightest snicker might set the gunman off. Thoughtless drunks though they were, they didn't want to be responsible for the kid's death.

"Wipe it off kid," the man leaning on the bar growled.

"With what, sir?" the kid was nearly weeping.

"Your shirt would do the trick."

The boy immediately unbuttoned his shirt and stripped it off. It snagged on the buckle of the gun belt and tore with a loud ripping sound. At that one of the bar-flies did snicker, but became dead silent at a cold glance from the gunslinger.

"Come on, kid, I'm tired of waiting."

The entire saloon fell so quiet the sound of a big blow-fly buzzing in a frantic circle in the saloon's front window seemed almost like a screaming wind.

The gunman's fingers tickled the grips of his pistol. The kid was sobbing now.

The bartender's eyes looked about to bulge from their sockets.

Then the unmistakable feel of cold steel pressed into the gunslinger's side.

Without a soul in the saloon noticing, the saddle tramp who'd been standing in the shadows at the end of the bar quietly nursing his whiskey had walked up beside the gunslinger.

While standing there, nearly out of the circle of light thrown by the hanging lamp he had seen the young boy come in. The boy had accidently bumped the gunfighter, causing him to spill whiskey on his boots. Now the man was prepared to kill the kid, simply because he could.

The saddle tramp bent close to the gunslinger's ear and said,

"Mister, you're going to apologize to this young man, and buy him a new shirt or I'm going to remove two of your ribs; a right and a left, and whatever's between them. Understand?"

The gunslinger nodded so vigorously his hat slid down over his eyes. "I'm sorry kid, honest I am! For real!"

The stunned kid looked at the saddle tramp, who said to the gunslinger, "Okay, now the gun, fingertips only."

The humiliated gunman upholstered his gun with two fingers and handed it over. The saddle tramp handed it to the bartender.

"Almost there." The saddle tramp nodded at the torn shirt the boy still held.

The fuming gunman handed the boy a five dollar bill.

The saddle tramp said, "Okay, get out of here, and don't come back!"

Fear lent wings to the feet of the gunfighter-turned-coward. The cowboys in the bar finally released their pent up laughter as he fled, leaving the swinging bat-wing doors creating a welcomed breeze behind him.

Later, when the ruckus had settled down and the last of the wobbly cowboys had stumbled out, the clumping of boot heels on the wooden sidewalk was replaced by the night sounds of crickets and an occasional far-off owl. As the bartender wiped down the bar, and trimmed the wicks on the lamps he asked the saddle tramp, "One for the road, my friend?"

"No thank you."

"Sure? It's on me. That was a fine thing you did for that boy earlier.

The saddle tramp nodded slightly, a small landslide of trail dirt sliding from his hat, and said, "I never could abide a bully. Good night my friend. I've got an appointment."

The bartender looked at him, puzzled.

"When I got to town, I stopped and arranged for the local barber to stay late and give me a haircut and shave." The saddle tramp paused and coughed a deep hacking cough, and spat a glob of red sputum into a bandana he then folded into a back pocket.

"Are you sure you don't want a drink? Sure sounds like you could use one?"

"No thank you my friend," the saddle tramp said, and shook the bartender's hand. "I have my own in my hotel room. I never leave home without it. I'll go there, have a large helping, and then hopefully get a good night's sleep. In the morning I'll have a hot bath, dress in my normal clothing, and board the stage for Tombstone. I have friends there I want to visit."

"What do you mean normal clothing?"

The saddle tramp smiled. There was blood on his teeth. "They say you can't tell a book by its cover. And often, that's a good thing. Again, good night my friend."

He walked toward the bat-wing doors.

The bartender said "Mister, I'd be proud to know your name. If you don't want no one to know you were here I won't tell. Promise."

The saddle tramp looked over his shoulder and said, "You can call me Doc." And he walked out.

The end

SAWBONES

"You're the sawbones?" Though it had to be a question, it was said more like a fiercely rude statement. The old doctor turned around as quickly as his advanced age would allow. He'd just finished examining a local man, a friend of his, killed in a gunfight, and was putting his signature on the death certificate.

A man he'd never seen before stood inside his office door glaring at him. The man hadn't knocked, simply barged in. His face wore a cocky smirk.

Though not normally a man to make snap judgments; the Doc immediately disliked him.

"The sign outside says Miles Bennell, M.D. I've also been called physician, healer, Doc, and a lady in Kansas even once called me an angel from Heaven after I saved her daughter from being choked to death by her own umbilical cord. And yes, I have been called a sawbones, but I find it more than a little degrading. Now, who are you?" The doctor squinted one eye, making one end of his handlebar mustache rise up in what under other circumstances might be comical. Though he was angered at being interrupted, he sensed that saying the wrong thing could be dangerous

The man's smirk grew, "I'm Hemp Buell. Get used to the name. You'll be hearing it a lot. I'm the new fastest gun west of the Rockies."

"Oh, that was you?"

"Yeah, that was me. I killed Jonas Regan. The man you just finished doing the last digging on"

Doc shook his head sadly. "You might spare the man a modicum of respect. Or, if not for him, for his family; his wife and two daughters, one born deaf as a stone; poor deaf little Eve. Jonas Regan was a farmer. He wasn't a gun fighter any more. He was an old man. He hadn't worn a gun in ten years. The biggest thing he'd killed in the last five was a mule deer for the table, and he did that with a rifle."

"He had a gun on when he came to town today."

"I know all about that. Everybody in town does. Everybody knows you threatened his family. And they all also know he was blind in one eye."

"I don't believe it."

"You better believe it, you cheap punk." The old doctor's eyes flared as he said it. "People around here liked Jonas Regan. The truth will spread every bit as fast as your new reputation."

Hemp Buell leaned close to Doc's face, his lip curled like a snarling dog. "You think you're so smart, don't you, old man? They'll be talking about me in every town in the territory. They'll be writing songs about me."

"A lot of dead men have songs written about them."

Buell grabbed Doc's lapels and screamed in his face, "I'll have a city named after me **Sawbones!**"

"More likely you'll have a cemetery named after you, because you'll be in one sooner than you think. Once word gets out that you got your reputation by killing a half blind old man they'll be lining up. All the wanna' be fastest guns. It won't be six months before you'll be on my table, or somebody else's for a signature on a death certificate. Then a pine box in Boot Hill. Then they might sing about you in saloons, but you'll never know it."

"We'll see who's right **Sawbones!**" Hemp Buell stormed out.

Eight weeks later:

Hemp Buell came to and looked up into the face of Doctor Miles Bennell. "What am I doing here **Sawbones**?"

"Nearly dying," Doc answered.

"Why here?"

"It was the most convenient place for you to nearly die."

"What's going on?"

"You met a faster gun," Doc told him.

"Am I going to die?"

"Everybody does."

"Damn you **Sawbones**! You think that's funny? What happened?" Buell lost his breath, gasping till he fell silent like a train running out of steam.

"The Deputy who brought you here told me what he knew of what happened. A cowboy who wanted to be the fastest gun in the West baited you to a cattle camp north of town by calling you a coward. Whether or not it was a fair fight he didn't know. The man was fast, but lucky for you, not a good shot. Instead of your chest or your gut, he got your left knee. That was yesterday afternoon. One of your friends found you this morning. You lay in a pile of cow manure all night, where they had dragged you behind a wagon. By this morning that knee had gotten started on a class-a infection. Your temperature was through the roof.

"So, now what?" Buell's eyelids drooped. "Drowsy. Can't hardly keep my eyes open." His voice was slurred, his tongue thick.

Doc looked down at him on the exam table, and thought about how recently he'd examined the lifeless body of Jonas Regan on the same table. An old man with a big hole in his chest and a widow and two daughters at home.

"I force-fed you some pills while you were out. A lot of them,"

"Well **Sawbones**! Are you just going to stand there and gloat about how wise you are? Or are you going to do something for me?" Buell had perfected wringing the worst from the derisive slur. Doc didn't answer. Instead he straightened and tightened the tourniquet he had himself long ago braided from the softest silk cord he could afford when he was a young man. Then he went about collecting a scalpel, needle, silk thread, bandages, and the other tools of his trade, sanitized them and arranged them neatly on a clean towel. He washed his hands thoroughly, then went to a cabinet and chose a tool that he detested using and only took out as an absolute last resort. Hemp's eyelids fluttered open when the cold alcohol splashed over his leg. When Doc laid a cloth over his face and poured chloroform on it, the bitter smell brought the realization of what was happening to Hemp Buell's clouded mind. Always a vicious man, the pain was sinking him to new levels of anger and hostility. He lurched up into a sitting position and grabbed at Doc's throat; not getting a grip, but leaving clearly visible finger-nail gouges on each side of the doctor's neck. Doc said, "For God's sake Buell, you've got enough laudanum in you to give a pony a good night's sleep. Now, just lay back and try to relax. Are you still in a lot of pain?" Hemp's forehead scrunched up in pain-addled thought. "Knee hurts real bad. Burns like fire. "Down below I can't feel it hardly 'tall. It's like my foot's gone. I looked down at it. I saw my toes stickin' outa' the bandages, so I know it's still there. They mostly look pasty white, but the nails look kinda' green. And I swear I can smell 'em, and they smell kinda' rank.

Doc said as compassionately as he could make himself, "Close your eyes and let the medicine do its work, I have some bones to saw."

"I'll see you in Hell **Sawbones**!"

Doc said, "There are more things in Heaven and Hell, Hemp Buell, than are dreamed of in your philosophy. I paraphrase."

Then he went about his business.

The end

SODBUSTER

As Newton Turner struggled to guide the plow, he tried vainly to mop rain and streaming mud from his eyes to clear his vision. As he did he recalled shading his eyes from glaring sun and wiping blowing silt away while he whipped stripes on Bess's flanks to get her to pull the plow through the same ground when it was baked hard as the bricks in the walls of the First National Bank of El Paso that sat just over six long, dusty miles to the West.

Though God knew Newt had no way to choose between the two, he spent more than a few sleepless nights tossing and twisting the sheets wondering how two such different curses could both be so all-fired miserable. When he'd talked Mister Jonas at the Feed and Grain into advancing him some seed corn the sky had dried up like God forgot how to make anything wetter than dust.

Then when he tried for wheat, the skies dropped every gallon that was left after Noah's voyage and the seed washed away like he'd never sewn it.

If not for the money he earned breaking his back for some of the bigger ranchers in the area, and an occasional helping hand in the way of a home-baked loaf of bread or a pie or jug of fresh milk from a neighbor the kids would be hungry and the place would again belong to First National of El Paso as it had before he and the kids had moved here from Las Cruces, New Mexico. To his surprise he'd discovered there were some Christians in Texas just like in New Mexico, despite everything Monica's parents had warned him of. He knew they didn't really suspect the entire rest of the world of being populated by heathens and sinners. They just didn't want to see their grandkids go; their last connection to their lost daughter.

After the flu had taken Monica there was nothing in the place for him but heartache around every corner. That they understood. Every time he stepped on a board that squeaked; that he hadn't fixed for her he hated himself a little. When he worked the pump handle and got more noise than water. When he pulled the ladder out of the barn to put on a fresh coat of red and two rungs were broken out. All the things he hadn't done for her.

Then when Swenson had offered him a fair price he'd packed up the kids and the few things that mattered most to them and taken off to become Texans.

On the road they saw a sign about a public auction in El Paso that looked promising.

They pulled their wagon into El Paso the morning of the sale, their travel poke getting light. Newt checked them into a hotel and inquired about the local bank. After arranging for an older lady who worked at the hotel to briefly keep an eye on the kids, he went to the bank and prearranged for a bank draft should he find he could afford to purchase the property being auctioned. It was just past a stage relay station about ten miles out of town.

The ranch wasn't large; barely a dozen acres. A strange crooked triangle shape, with a slightly odd notch in the north-west corner, it didn't seem to hide anything shady, but didn't show much indication of water on the surveyor's map. Monica had always preached at him to have faith in the Lord. No, preach was too strong a word. She wanted it of him; so faith he would have. He bid on the ranch, not expecting to win, and it was theirs.

Once they moved in, Newt worked constantly at making the old place a paying concern; as well as making the property a pleasant and livable homestead where he and the children could have a new life. Then there was the drought, and then the downpour and Newt found himself sitting at the kitchen table trying to explain to six-year old Bethany and ten-year old Johnny that things weren't going very well. The one thing that had turned out to be a Godsend about their small spread outside of El Paso, Texas was the clear and steady running stream only forty yards from the house. It wasn't enough water to be of any use for irrigation during the dry spells; Newt would have spent so much time hauling water he wouldn't have time to work the crop. But Beth loved carrying pitchers of water to the small patch of dirt beside the porch where she was trying diligently to cultivate a garden.

Mama's garden she called it. She couldn't have picked a worse patch of earth on the entire parcel of ground; more rock than soil. But Mama's garden was next to the porch back home, so that's where it must be.

Blond and blue eyed, little Bethy could charm the bark off the trees without hardly trying. She was so sweet that in no time at all the neighbors were giving her clippings, snippings, bulbs, and even a full bush or two.

Miss Joanne Roy, her nearest neighbor gave her a large mum which she helped her plant and showed her how to care for. She showed Bethy how to pinch off the blooms and told her the right time of year to do it. It tried hard to grow. After a while some of the more far-away neighbors took to riding several miles to bring Bethy flowers and plants they knew she'd like. Even a few vegetables that hadn't had a prayer. Everybody was rooting for Bethy and her little garden. Sadly, just like the fields that her daddy worked so hard to turn into a farm, mostly all she grew was rocks, though she did manage to get a surprisingly bright and stout twist of pink and violet morning glories popping from the dirt a foot from the porch and climbing the post holding up the porch roof. Johnny laughed at the vines, like a big brother would be expected to.   He called them weeds, and said that it would be hard not to grow morning glories. The real trick would be to keep them from growing.

Newt sat on the edge of the porch, gathered Bethy on his lap and said, "Bethy, don't you pay any attention to your big brother. I don't know what we'd be doing if not for your morning glories. We'd be in a real fix. It's those morning glories that are holding that old post up. It's plain as day. Our porch roof would have been down on our heads by now, sure as shootin' if not for your flowers. Plus, they're beautiful. And honey, I'm real proud of how hard you've worked on your garden. And your mama would be real proud, too."

Bethy's perfect baby-blues looked up into his soul and she said, "It's Mama's garden too Daddy."

Newt slid Beth off his lap. When she was solidly planted on both feet he gave her a light swat on the butt and said, "Go tell Johnny to get washed up for dinner."

From behind him he heard "I'll get washed up Pa." Then in a softer, very different voice, "I'm proud of you too, Bethy."

He'd had no idea Johnny was still nearby. But the exchange both surprised and thrilled him. He'd had at least a dozen well-meaning friends try to advise him on the upcoming trials of being both a father and a mother. So far, no matter how hard he tried, he'd felt like a dismal failure. Then Johnny's one sentence warmed him inside like a coal stove that had broken the deep down blistering cold that had been wrapped around his heart on this long terrible stormy night. A heat he needed. Because the cold it broke was an evil thing that could cause him irreparable harm if not caught in time.

So now they sat at the dinner table, nibbling at a meal made up primarily of gifts from generous neighbors; charity Newt would have been way too proud to have accepted back in what he considered his other life, and some special treats like some hard candy and chocolates Newt picked up for the kids after helping Mister Jonas unload two wagons of merchandise from St. Louis that morning. They were not the norm, and he would watch them brush their teeth before bedtime. It was time to discuss the sad money situation with them. They wouldn't understand. Things were already tough, and could get tougher. He hoped the sweets would soften the blow.

He was incredibly proud of the kids when they gratefully ate the stew made with the jack-rabbit he'd prevented from dining on Bethy's morning glories as the sun was rising that dawn. The kids were so used to his shooting at possible meals they didn't even take notice of the shots while sleeping any more. Ammunition was something else Mister Jonas was kind enough to pay him with from time to time.

He tried to explain to them as simply as possible that hard work doesn't always mean things will go your way. That was why they were so fortunate to have such good friends. He said that someday something would happen that would bring them a grubstake. Bethy laughed at that, and Johnny said, "That would be great. We haven't had steak in a long time."

"No, son, not that kind of steak, unfortunately. At least not yet; but some day. He paused and pulled his kid's chairs up next to him, one on either side. Grub - s t a k e, he spelled it out. It's an old miner's term. It means getting-by money, money to get by on till you strike it rich."

Bethy asked, "Is that what we're gonna' do daddy, strike it rich?"

"It would be nice Darlin', but for right now I'd be happy if with just struck it not-poor'."

Johnny asked, "Do you know where we can get a grubstake Pa?"

"No I don't son and I could sure use some of your mom's faith right now."

Newt glanced out the window at Bethy's morning glories wrapped around the cracked old porch post. He recalled once telling the kids over a breakfast of corncakes with maple syrup tapped from a tree on the far side of a neighbor's field, with the neighbor's approval, that if just one thing came out of the ground on this place it would be a miracle; and a sign from God that they would make it.

Later as the kids were saying their prayers, they heard a horse galloping hard, coming closer to the one-room cabin, fast. The unknown rider reined the horse in just outside and things fell quiet. Newt put his finger to his lips and motioned for the kids to stay put. He began walking to the door. Before he'd made three strides someone began pounding impatiently. Newt began walking again, adjusting his path slightly in the direction of his rifle. He hadn't gone two more steps before the person on the other side kicked the door so hard it trembled in its frame. Johnny yelped. Bethy began bawling. Newt started toward the door again, his fist cocked, ready to face whoever was on the other side. The unknown person kicked the door again. This second kick was too much for the old wood. The door swung open wide. Before Newt could throw his punch the man who had kicked it open stepped through and leveled a gun at his forehead. Helpless, and fearing for his children, Newt could do nothing but raise his hands.

The man holding the gun looked around. He stared hard at Johnny and Bethy still kneeling beside their beds and said, "Oh, Christian' folks. That's good. Non-violent folks are easy to deal with; a lot less trouble.

You a sodbuster, are ya'?"

"Tryin'," Newt answered. "Who are you?" He struggled to hold his temper in check.

The man with the gun shrugged and his left shoulder came down bloody.

"You don't need to know who I am, only what I'll do, prayin' sodbuster. There's a posse on my trail. If they show up here, you're going to tell them you haven't seen a soul in weeks. If you do that maybe you and your cute little youngn's will be all right. You understand?"

Though not a worldly man by any stretch of the imagination, Newt had been in his share of scrapes, and immediately sensed that to show weakness to this man would be a big mistake. Looking away from the man, Newt told the kids to climb into bed then went straight to them and gave each one a kiss and then walked back to the evil stranger. He looked the man with the gun straight in the eyes, almost as though they were having a staring contest. But if so the stranger knew from the start he was the loser. There must have been something in Newt's eyes that wasn't to his liking; because Newt stepped toward him, and though he didn't lower the gun he moved it aside just a little.

When they were nearly nose to nose, Newt said, "I don't know who you are, but you ought to know; the Bible is full of stories about men that killed people who threatened their families. Mister, I don't much care what you do to me, but if you hurt my kids, I'll cut your head off and stomp it into the ground.

Newt was already praying in preparation for meeting his maker and seeing Monica. But instead of pulling the trigger, the man screamed furiously and clubbed at Newt with the gun.

Newt dodged left, and recalling the blood that had soaked the left shoulder of the man's coat after he'd shrugged it up against his head, threw a looping right at the area of his left ear. His punch connected solidly. The man's scream of pain dwarfed his previous scream of rage. He fell over backwards like he'd been shot, losing his grip on the gun as he fell. It clattered to the cabin's board floor. Now, both kids were bawling their heads off, hiding under their covers.

Thanking the Lord the lamp hadn't been knocked from the table and was still lit, Newt told them, "Hush, everything will be all right. Daddy will tuck you in proper in just a few minutes."

The man on the floor was crawling toward the gun, reaching for it; still moaning and cursing Newt the whole time for what he'd done to him. Newt wasn't a cruel man. It was something he'd always prided himself on. He even felt guilty when he killed game for the table, though he knew they needed it desperately for food. But this animal had threatened his kids. This was different. When the man was nearly close enough to reach the gun, Newt brought his foot down hard on his hand. Both the crunch and the resulting scream were satisfying.

Newt went to check on the kids. His attention was diverted for less than a minute. When he turned back the criminal was on his feet, stumbling out the door, waving the gun around in their direction with his uninjured hand. It was clearly strange to him, but nothing to mess with all the same.

He turned right off the porch and ran toward the corner of the house. Newt grabbed the lamp in one hand and his rifle in the other and followed.

Newt couldn't see the man once he was out the door, but he could hear him blundering around through the darkness. The criminal really was luckier than he deserved. The virtually nonexistent rainfall had kept even the weeds from growing so he didn't have much foliage to fight with, but Newt could hear the man's feet dragging through the dry silt, and the ragged wheezing of his breath in the hot night air. And while he was running in the dark, Newt knew every inch of the sunbaked yard like the back of his hand. Then he heard a thump and a thrashing, accompanied by a combination of whining and cursing; the foulest curses Newt had ever heard; growing in volume with every word. Newt lifted the lantern. Most of the curses were directed at him, but nearly as many were aimed at the morning glories wrapped like a snake around the ankles of the gunman laid out face down on the ground, flailing around like a landed fish. Newt walked up to him and pressed his rifle against the small of the man's back.

"What's happenin' Pa?" Johnny stood looking over the porch railing with Bethy tucked protectively behind him.

"Nothing son, this man just tripped. You two go back to bed. Us two are going to stay out here for a little while and have a talk. Isn't that right?" He prodded the fallen man in the back with the muzzle of the rifle.

The man grunted around a mouthful of dirt.

"What are you gonna' talk about?" Bethy asked.

"I don't know, Hun. Maybe about Christian sodbusters."

"The door's broke Pa," Johnny pointed out. "I don't think it'll close."

"I know son. I'll fix it up tomorrow. You two go on now."

The kids hurried inside.

"You're quite a man." The new voice startled Newt as much as it did the criminal on the ground. But the criminal began crying. 'What now?' Newt thought. He was glad the kids had made it inside before whatever was happening now. With the ruckus going on he hadn't heard a horse ride in. He looked up. Standing at the corner of the house, just in the light of the lamp stood a man with his thumbs hooked casually in his gun belt.

Before Newt could ask, the stranger introduced himself; "Benjamin Jackson, Deputy Sheriff of El Paso County." He pointed to the badge on his vest by way of confirmation. "I've been following this man for three days. He robbed a stage, and killed the driver, and maybe the shotgun guard. We don't know about him for sure yet. He's in awful bad shape. But he got a shot off before he went down. A passenger said it took this man's left ear off. He prodded the criminal hard in the ribs with the toe of his boot. I'll take him off your hands now. And you've apprehended a murderer who was fleeing justice. You've just earned yourself a thousand dollar reward.

When Newt finally got to tuck his kids in, Johnny asked him, "What really happened Pa?"

"We got our grubstake son."

Bethany asked, "Did we strike it rich Daddy?"

"No Darlin', but we did strike it 'not-poor'. And now we know your morning glories really are a miracle."

The end

SHOTGUN GUARD

Gage Branch opened his eyes and held them that way for as long as he could before letting them drift closed. It seemed like holding them open for that brief moment had sapped nearly all the strength his body had in it. In that moment he'd seen only an unfamiliar ceiling that was in need of a coat of paint; white, if the plan was to match what was already there. Apparently there had been a meeting where a great many flies had congregated up there and each had left its mark to be remembered by. As far as where he was; all he could tell was that he was lying on a table. After a moment's rest he rolled his eyes around and saw a small room with walls the same color as the ceiling, but based upon first impressions, not such strangers to a paint brush.

His first attempt at movement, beyond moving his eyes around enough to survey a small portion of the room, consisted of nothing more than trying to lift his head. He was rewarded with the wickedest pain of his life, and he'd dealt with some considerable wicked pain in his life so far. Ten Gauge had decided long ago never to say that any pain was the worst of his whole life, 'cause his whole life wasn't over yet. But the way this hurt; he wasn't so sure that was true this time. Of one thing there was no doubt at all; this was his wickedest pain so far. The pain had been vague; spread all over the upper half of his body, but in the brief instant before he grayed out and everything turned black, he glimpsed a framed certificate on one wall. His vision was too blurry to distinguish anything but the letters M. D. after a printed name that was probably easy as pie reading for anyone who didn't just wake up feeling like they'd had a hot poker shoved through their chest.

How long it was before he opened his eyes again he had no idea. As it turned out, he later learned it was overnight, which brought it to a period of three days since a man with a bandanna over his face had tried to bring both his career and his life to a premature end.

When he next tried to open his eyes he found it impossible. They felt as though they were glued closed. He'd have been quite embarrassed to know the glue that held them was nothing more than tears. He feared for a panicky moment that maybe some parts of his body had given up and died before the whole package was ready to give up. When he tried to bring up his right hand to pry his eyes open the horrible agony that passing out had spared him of for a while returned with a vengeance.

"Here, you lie still, let me give you a hand." It was a pleasant voice; both pleasantly female, and pleasantly young. The pleasant voice began humming softly, soothingly, and presently he felt a soft cloth damp with the smell of brine begin wiping gently at his eyes. After a moment she said, "Try now.

Both eyes opened on the first try. After a few blinks, and a little effort; nothing more than shaking off the cobwebs of a long night's sleep or a mild hangover he could see fine. He looked up at the owner of the voice. She asked, "How does everything look now?" She stood on his left, wringing out the cloth with which she'd wiped his eyes.

"Beautiful."

"My granddaughter has that effect on many of my male patients. You're a very lucky man to be able to wake up and see anything. " An elderly man with a big handlebar moustache stood on his right.

"Did something happen to my eyes?" Gage sounded panicky.

"No, I'm sorry. I didn't mean you were lucky to see. I meant you were lucky to wake up. I didn't think that was going to happen for a while. You took a.45 slug to the chest, and one to the shoulder. The shoulder one was through-and-through, fortunately for you. It just clipped the bone. Another inch and you might never have been able to lift your right arm again. The one in the chest was much worse. It lodged in your right lung. But you were lucky."

"It doesn't sound like one of my luckiest days."

The old man lowered his head. "Mister Branch, your driver was killed. You've been here in my office for three days, surprising me every time I came in the room and found you still alive. I'd like to take the credit for your survival, but the fact is, the only reason you're not six feet under is because of a dentist."

"What?"

"Yes, there was a dentist on the stage with you. One of the other passengers; a lady salesperson from Chicago said he washed his hands with whiskey from a flask he had in his satchel and then took an instrument that, based on her description, sounded like a tooth extractor, from the satchel and dug the bullet out of your chest. He then packed the hole with cotton just like he'd pulled a tooth, and wrapped gauze around your chest, while the saleslady assisted; without vomiting. She was justifiably proud of that. You were fortunate he had his bag with him. Luckily the bullet wasn't in very deep. A rib slowed it down. It meant I spent an extra hour picking out bone fragments. But the stage line's paying; so don't give it a second thought. Still any hole in the lung is serious. His side-of-the-road surgery definitely kept you alive till I could stitch you up properly. She said he then sat in the stage and sipped whiskey from the flask and playing solitaire between coughing fits till a passing farmer rode for help. Then you were brought here."

"And here is your office."

"Right; Miles Bennell, M. D. And the young lady who helped you open your eyes is Tally, my sometime nurse, and fulltime granddaughter."

"Three days ago, that was?"

Tally, the part-time nurse, and full-time granddaughter answered, "Yes three. I'll bet you're getting hungry by now." Then she asked as an afterthought, "Is your name really Ten Gauge?"

Gage couldn't help but smile through the pain. Part of it, he supposed was because the question was asked by such a beauty. "No, it's really Gage Branch. My father was a shotgun guard for years. My mother said as soon as I was born and he knew I was a boy he decided I was to be named Gage so he could call me Ten Gauge after the gun he carried when he rode the stage. It's a nickname. I don't think she minded. He loved the job. They're both gone now. I don't suppose most people know there are two different spellings of the word. So I sort of grew up into the job. When the stage line offered it I took it. And yeah, I'm kinda' hungry. "

The doctor said to Tally, "Why don't you get our patient some soup, Tally? Maybe we'll see if he feels up to sitting up, with a little help. He's no doubt a bit worn out. He's not only been out of commission for three days but he also performed surgery just before his own trauma."

Tally left the room.

Gage looked at the doctor, puzzled. "What are you talking about?"

"Well, according to both the Chicago saleslady and the dentist, after the robber shot you twice, you still got off a shot that amputated his left ear. Don't you remember that?"

Gage squinted for a moment before answering. "I do now" He looked disappointed.

"What's wrong?"

"I was trying to amputate his head. Tom Taylor was my best friend," Gage said, referring to the dead stage driver.

Doc nodded. "I can understand that. Furnace is just a wide spot in a dirt road right now, compared to El Paso, just like a hundred other little towns in Texas trying hard to grow into a big town. And the stage transfer station is what the town had to grow around in the beginning. Everybody here knew Tom. If you'd been awake last night you'd have heard the ruckus when the deputy sheriff had to break up the necktie party some of our citizens had planned for the man whose ear you removed."

"So did the party come off as planned?"

"No, the deputy managed to calm them down. It was a near thing. He's currently locked up in the back room of the stage depot. We don't have a jail. I feel confident that man will get his neck stretched, but it will be done lawfully. With two witnesses and missing an ear by way of identification, I don't think his chances of getting off are very good. The trial is set for next Friday; that's five days from now, in El Paso. "

"Will I be out of here?"

"You better be. You're the star witness."

Doc paused for a moment, and then asked, "Gage, was it a gold shipment?"

"No Doc. They try their best to keep the schedules secret. Just the two passengers this trip. But I sure am glad one of them was a dentist"

Doc said quietly, "One man dead, and another man nearly dead for nothing. Then he called out "Tally, let's get that soup into our patient, then get him off this table and into a proper bed in the other room so he can recuperate."

Tally came in with a bowl of soup.

Gage said, "I don't know if I can walk."

Tally said, "That's all right, the table has wheels on it."

Gage cautiously shook his head. "Doc, you better get me outta' your office pretty quick; I could get to likin' it here, too much. And I want to meet this dentist that saved my life."

"Too late, I'm afraid. He left the morning after the robbery. He said with lay-overs he still had three days ahead of him on the stage."

"Going where?"

"Tombstone."

"One more thing?" Gage said."

What's that?"

Your town's name; why Furnace?"

"We had a heat wave once, about forty years ago. I was the only one in town who had a thermometer. Even though it was the kind that was made to be inside of a person, not outside of a building I set it outside on my windowsill. It never went under a hundred and three for a week and a half. If the town was a patient it would have been dead and buried. That's when we decided two things; on a name for the town, and that Furnace was never going to become the ghost-town that a lot of little western towns had. And it never has," he added proudly.

"Sounds like you're a stubborn group."

"That we are. And most of those ghost towns popped up because of mines; gold or silver. Or because people thought they were going to get rich finding gold or silver. Once the precious metal or the dreams ran out the town died. Around here, it's all farms and ranches. And the businesses that make up the town that grew to serve the farmers and ranchers. The land is what you're willing to make of it. If you're blessed with enough rain and a strong back you can survive. Furnace has survivors.

While Gage sipped his soup, he and Tally chatted. He learned a little about the ninety-seven people, give-or-take who made up Furnace. And he learned that though he'd missed the dentist who'd saved his life, the Chicago saleslady was staying at the town's only boarding house till the trial, so he might get a chance to introduce himself to her when he wasn't gushing blood. Gage told her that if he'd known the people in Furnace were so hospitable he'd have asked to be on this run sooner.

To which Tally replied, "I don't know; it doesn't seem to have been very good for your health, so far."

Gage shrugged, and it hurt; but still he managed a smile. "Sometimes you just gotta' roll the dice."

Three nights later Gage felt up to joining Tally and Doctor Bennell for dinner at Furnace's only restaurant; 'The Chuck Wagon'. Just as they were finishing up with coffee a very attractive lady in an eastern looking dress walked in, and stopping, looked around the room. After a moment she crossed to where Gage sat and said, "So, this is what you look like with your eyes open." She fluttered her big brown eyes and smiled as she said it, then stood beside his chair with her hand on his shoulder.

"You're the Chicago saleslady I presume." He answered and returned her smile.

"Yes, Mattie Drew; dealer in silk fineries, formerly of Chicago; headed for El Paso, till things got interrupted."

She then looked at Doc and repeated her name, also with a big smile.

He said hello and gave her a small polite smile in return.

She then gave Tally a brief glance and said, "Hello." But it was said without repeating her name, and with the power level on the smile turned down a bit. Tally returned her hello, but not the smile.

After dinner she walked Gage back to her grandfather's office, where she'd convinced the doctor Gage should reside till the trial. It was something she'd decided she should do once she saw Mattie Drew on the street a couple days after the stage robbery. For his own good, of course. After all; with what he'd been through, shouldn't he have the best care close at hand, if he needed it?

And the handful of souls who made up the wide spot in the road called Furnace, Texas awaited the trial.

The end

SALOON GIRL

Wanda tried her best to melt into the shadows in the back of the Saguaro Saloon. It wasn't easy. The shadows were few and small. On Saturday nights the owner kept the place lit up like Christmas. It wasn't even a typical Saturday night. On top of all the ranch hands and cow-pokes that had drawn their pay, a cattle drive was camped just a few miles north of town. So all the regular rowdies were pushing and shoving with a bunch of new rowdies who were just as determined to claim that one open spot at the bar, or that one empty chair at a table. Or one of the girls the saloon employed to provide company for the cowboys. The girls were paid to talk along, laugh along, and drink along. The rule of the house was simple; a happy cowboy was a drinking cowboy. So keep them smiling, and happy and drinking.

Tonight Wanda's smiles came hard, or not at all. So she tried hard to hide. It wasn't an easy thing to do for the prettiest girl in a room full of cowhands; each looking for a pretty girl to have a good time with.

No, not easy at all. But she simply couldn't do the job tonight; no, not this night.

A drunken cowboy came staggering up to the bar and slammed the palm of his hand down on the scarred, beer soaked surface. It was a move intended as much to save himself from a fall to the floor as to get the bartender's attention; but he accomplished both.

Sam, the owner and bartender, walked down to where he stood. "What'll it be, friend?"

The man slammed his empty shot glass on the bar top by way of answer. Sam filled the glass with rye.

Then the cowboy leaned over the bar toward Sam and whispered like a kid with a secret, "What's wrong with Wanda?"

He nodded to where she stood as far back in a corner of the room as she could get with her shoulders hunched as if sheltering from an invisible wind.

Sam shook his head "She's a classic example of a nice girl taken in by the wrong guy. About six months ago a smooth talking gambler hit town. He came in regular for about a week. He spent most of his time acting like Wanda really meant something to him. He told her she was the most beautiful woman he'd ever seen, which was probably true. He claimed that he was going to be rich, so rich that he wouldn't be able to spend it all himself. He'd have more money than any one person could ever spend. He was going to have so much money he'd be able to wave it to fan himself when he was hot in the summer and burn it to stay warm in the winter."

"And you heard him say all this?"

Sam nodded. "Every word turned my stomach, too. I really like Wanda. She's a nice girl."

The cowboy said, somewhat sadly, "Sounds like a real lowlife."

"That's just about right," Sam agreed, "and of course he just couldn't go on living without her as his wife."

"You mean she's married?"

"For now," Sam answered. The thing he didn't tell her was that his plan for getting rich was robbing a stage. There was a trial in El Paso yesterday. After nine am Monday she'll be a widow."

The cowboy got a look on his face like he was digging deep in his brain for a thought that was buried there. "Well," he said finally. "Who knows? Maybe it's for the best. My grandma used to say, "The Lord wanders in strange ways performin' mysteries, or somethin' like that."

Sam said, "I don't think you've got that just right, pal, but I get the idea."

The end

Silk Fineries & Sweet Sixteen

On this December twentieth evening the cold wind blowing off the prairie strongly contradicted the name hung on the town in the dead of a miserable, sweltering summer a lot of years before. The wind made a variety of sounds as it passed around and through the wooden structures of Furnace, Texas. It whistled, it moaned, it screamed, and it made the buildings rattle. Some of the oldest and frailest of them shook on their stone foundations.

But behind the spotless front window of the shop called 'Silk Fineries' that sat on the town's main street right across from the stage depot, the kerosene lamps burned bright. On a table usually used for displaying ladies dresses and accessories there was a prettily decorated cake with sixteen candles; their light not as bright, but a lot more festive.

The shop was closed. The only one inside was Wanda; saloon girl turned seamstress. She'd stayed late to decorate and prepare the cake for the arrival of the guest of honor and her family and friends. They were due any minute. She had no doubt the biting wind and blowing sand were making it hard to see to guide the wagon the short distance into town. She'd cleared the counter to make space for presents. While she waited she decided to add some wood to the stove to make sure the shop was toasty warm. As she did, a soft rap came at the back door of the shop. Wanda went to the door and let in Doctor Bennell and Tally. Tally carried several packages wrapped in brightly colored paper and tied with ribbon. After Tally placed the presents on the counter, and while Doc was putting coffee on the stove, Wanda slipped a gift she'd made from under the counter and placed it on top with the others. After the trial in El Paso it wasn't long before she knew she couldn't go on drinking with strangers, laughing on command, and pretending to care about staying alive.

During the brief time that Mattie Drew originally viewed as being trapped in Furnace awaiting the trial, she'd gotten to meet and come to know enough of the town's citizens to decide that she really didn't want to trade the big city turmoil of Chicago for the big city turmoil of El Paso after all.

The ladies of Furnace had been excited to see an establishment like Silk Fineries come to town. But it quickly became obvious that except for the wives and daughters of some of the bigger ranchers nobody in the area could afford to purchase such luxuries. Still, everybody from the average farmer or cowboy to the wealthiest landowner occasionally needed clothing repaired or altered. Even a millionaire can split his pants. So in addition to the silk items which still came in from Chicago there were jeans and shirts, and even aprons. When she'd begun making dresses to order from the pattern and fabric the customer chose, sometimes taking barter in payment, she'd gotten too busy to handle it herself. So Wanda had fit in like the right piece in a puzzle. She'd had some of the necessary skills, and what she didn't know she'd picked up quickly with Mattie's instruction.

Finally, over the howling of the wind, as Doc was pouring his third cup of coffee and Wanda was checking the clock for at least the tenth time, they heard the sound of a buckboard pulling to a stop behind the shop. Wanda hurried to the door and opened it, propping her hip against it to fight the wind, so it didn't get away from her.

Doc stepped up behind her and reached over her head and added his weight to the door.

The Turner family entered; Newt, the farmer from New Mexico, who had pulled up stakes and moved with his children to the middle of nowhere to start over when all his other options were gone. It was something he wouldn't have had the guts to do without the memory of Monica's faith in his head. Then Mattie; who came to Furnace Mattie Drew. She'd literally bumped into Newt on the street one day, and five weeks later become Mattie Turner. She adapted from Chicago saleslady to Texas ranch life amazingly well. And equally well to the position of stepmother. Johnny came in next. Now twenty, he'd taken a lot of the work load off his father's back. He was a great help on the ranch that was not huge but had grown steadily since the night of the astonishing windfall that had come by way of a reward ten years before. Last, but not least came Bethany, the adorable six-year-old whose morning glories put an end to the escape of a one eared stage robber; now grown into a beautiful young woman of sixteen. She was totally surprised when everyone shouted "HAPPY BIRTHDAY!"

Later they had some unexpected guests; Deputy Jackson knocked on the door and Sam even closed the saloon early and came along with him. Sam said, "Nobody comes in on Monday anyway. And Bethy is only going to turn sixteen once."

"Deputy Jackson asked "Any cake left?"

Later, after cake was eaten and the presents were opened friends and family sat and talked.

Sam said, "A lot of things happened in the last ten years because of a botched stage robbery." Then he looked at Wanda, and said, "sorry darlin'."

Wanda said, "That's okay. I'm better off. I might never have realized it if it hadn't happened. And I get more beauty sleep." She laughed and everyone laughed along.

"Well, after that the county decided I needed a real office," Deputy Jackson said, one with a cell; to hold off lynch mobs if nothing else." He paused, and then continued, "The good news is I haven't had to lock anybody up in six months. I must be doing something right."

"I never doubted you for a minute, Benjamin." Doc said.

"Hey Doc", Newt asked "Are you really planning on hangin' it up."

"Yes. As of March first Doctor John will be taking over my practice."

"He's the young guy you introduced around when I was out of town buying cattle?"

"That's the man. He's twenty-two years old and wants to move from Dallas where there are currently twenty-four practicing physicians to Furnace where there is currently one. He's less than a year and a half out of school. He's very qualified, and my patients who met him seemed to like him."

Bethany said, "I think he's handsome."

Newt said, "Twenty-two is way too old Bethy."

Bethany pooched out her lower lip and rolled her eyes at Mattie, playing the 'us girls gotta' stick together' card. It didn't work. Mattie took Newt's hand and gave Bethy a tiny shake of her head.

Shifting back to the subject of the new doctor, Sam asked, "Doc if you don't mind my askin' is he buying the practice and the building? Will his office still be where yours is?"

"Yes, Sam. You won't have to search for a new doctor's office if you've imbibed in too much of your own product," Doc answered good-naturedly. "And what is more important to the good people of Furnace is that he intends to continue employing Tally as his nurse. Though he was a little disappointed to learn she was married. Especially to a man who makes his living with a shotgun."

"Where is Gage, Tally, on a run?" Mattie asked

"Yes. He made me promise to save him a piece of cake. So you behave yourself," she scolded Deputy Jackson, who was eyeing up a third piece.

"Where's the boy?" Sam asked.

 "Little Gage is at a school friend's birthday party. He said to tell you happy birthday Bethy."

"Tell him I said thanks," she said, beaming.

"Furnace definitely is changing," Doc said. "We're getting new people all the time. We have our own bank. And the town well's finally deep enough to not dry up every summer. And then adding onto the school last year." He paused and nodded toward the far edge of town, unseen in the distance. "And that steeple going up on the church is really going to be something to see."

Johnny Turner took the last bite of his cake, and wincing, grabbed his jaw and said, "What we really need around here is a dentist. But I guess there's no chance of that ever happening."

Doc said, "I don't know. You never know who might step off that stage."

The end

A HANDFUL OF HOLIDAY STORIES

"A THANKSGIVING CAROL"

Stave 1

Trillion Kane was famous; one of the world's most well-known and popular rock stars. This must be understood, or nothing wonderful can come of the story I'm going to relate.

Trillion looked down at the mirror that held the line of coke. Last one, he thought. It was hard to believe. He knew which one would be his last, but he couldn't remember his first. It was a long time ago. Back when scrounging the cash for each line was a challenge. Back when each line seemed a personal triumph.

Now money was no object. Now he could buy the stuff by the pound if he wanted. Now he could afford his own cocaine factory if he wanted. Now he could afford to buy just about anything in the world that he might want. This was what he struggled for all those years; success, money, the power to have anything he wanted, whenever he wanted it.

He had it, and it didn't matter.

He slid the rolled up hundred dollar bill across the mirror and the fat line of powder disappeared up his nose like it had never been there.

'Now you see it, now you don't.'

I missed my calling, Trillion thought. All those years I spent hammering a Les Paul when what I really got good at was making cocaine disappear. I should have been a magician. 'Gather round folks.' See two thousand dollars' worth of illegal pharmaceutical product inhaled like expensive air. All for the joy of a nose full of blood and a head that felt like an over-inflated basketball, just to get through the day, and then to face another miserable day, and suck up more the following night.

The phone rang, the sound piercing Trillion's skull like a blunt knife. He wobbled to his feet and stumbled to the phone at the end of the couch.

"Trillion?"

"Yeah," he muttered, sniffing as he spoke.

"Man, you sound rough." It was Dave, his manager.

"What do you want, Dave?"

"The show; The MTV interview," Dave said, his voice carrying a suggestion of thinly-veiled anger.

"What about it?"

"Man that was bad, even for MTV."

"Bad how?" Trillion mumbled, his mouth filled with cotton.

Dave snickered through the phone; a snicker devoid of humor. "Bad how! You were there! You don't remember?"

Trillion rubbed his eyes and leaned against the wall. "That was way back yesterday. That was a long time ago."

"That's very funny. I kill myself to get you these interviews and you go on the air and blow it. I got a call ten minutes ago from their programming manager and he wasn't calling to say thanks. He said that if it hadn't been live it would have never been aired. As it is we'll be lucky not to get sued. Thank God there was somebody with a finger on the time-delay button to block the worst of it."

"What did I do?"

Dave was silent for a moment. "You really don't remember? Did you record it?"

"No."

"Listen, Chuck," Dave said evenly. Dave was one of the few who knew Trillion's real name, and only used it when he felt it was necessary to get his full attention, like a parent using their child's full name to scold them. "You better get it together, and quick. The new album's due to release in less than a month and you're still three songs short. Then you go on MTV and come off as a whiny, burned out, spoiled brat. You've got what half the guys in the world would give their right arm for and you complain about it."

"What did I say?"

"You don't remember? You really don't?"

Trillion's silence spoke volumes.

"Well I recorded it, but if I watched it again I'd either quit as your manager or…"

"Or what?" Trillian growled; his cotton-mouth now tasting like it was full of vinegar.

"Never mind." Dave paused, the pause filled by a hopeless sigh. "Just never mind. I'll send over a copy of the disc. You watch it if you want, or don't, it's all the same to

me. The way you're going there won't be any career to manage soon, and you can go back to playing one-nighters in bars, like you were when I found you."

"What do you mean by that?"

"Nothing, Chuck. It's just that back then you were a nice kid with a lot of talent but without all the baggage. That's what I liked about you. That's why I took you on."

"You took me on!" Trillion snarled. The sound of his own voice hurt his head, and his vision doubled. He leaned on the table for support. "You're lucky I let you get a piece of me. I'm the star, and don't you forget it. You were just as much of a nobody as I was when we met; a two-bit agent with a half dozen has-beens or never-weres working dives. I'm the only one that ever got a recording contract, and it's me that paid for that Porsche you tool around in, and don't forget it."

"Yeah Chuck, you're right. We started out together. You were the smiling, personable, talented rocker, and I was the agent busting my hump to help you. The difference is I still take my job seriously." The phone clicked in Trillion's ear, then silence.

"Hey! Don't you hang up on me! You can't! You can't!" A mechanical voice came from the receiver, telling him that if he'd like to make a call, please hang up and try again. It was more than he could handle. The phone sailed across the room and hit the TV, instantly sending a jagged spider of cracks across the screen. Acrid tendrils of smoke curled from the air slots atop the set. Trillion stared at the ruined TV, then turned and looked around the room. His blurred gaze fell on the bag of coke. His stomach clutched and he went stumbling for the bathroom, caroming off of furniture and walls as he went. He barely made it to the bathroom and fell to his knees, banging his forehead on the front of the toilet tank. His stomach clutched up again and what felt like everything he'd eaten since his first birthday splashed in the toilet. Just as the heaving eased, he got a whiff of what he'd deposited in the bowl and it started all over again. It seemed to go on forever, till his vision blurred again, his eyes rolled back and he flopped to the tile floor like a landed fish.

Stave 2

When he awoke it was obvious he'd vomited again while he was passed out. His shirt was a mess and he could feel it crusted on his chin and cheek. Trillion rolled onto his back. His head was a little clearer, and the thought hit him that he'd been lucky to pass out on his side. If he'd been on his back he might have choked to death on his own vomit like so many other famous rockers had.

Yeah; lucky. Right. Foolish thought, considering what he'd intended to do ever since he got up this morning. Wobbling to his feet, Trillion grabbed a towel and wiped the worst of the vomit from his chin. He splashed a little water on his face and slowly walked to the bedroom. The etched glass mirror on the dresser seemed to dare him to look at himself, but he stared at the floor as he pulled open the top drawer, shuffled aside the socks stored there, and took out the revolver.

It was small but nasty looking, blued steel and black grips. His hand shook as he lifted the gun and put the snub-nosed barrel in his mouth. It shook so badly that the steel rattled against his teeth, the sound echoing through his throbbing head. He closed his eyes and slowly pulled back the hammer till it clicked, the sharp sound making him jump. His finger slowly squeezed the trigger. At the last second, before he applied enough pressure to remove the top of his head, Trillion opened his eyes and looked in the mirror.

Someone stood behind him.

Trillion spun around, a frightened whimper escaping his lips. The motion staggered him and his hip hit the edge of the dresser, slamming the mirror against the wall and starting a cascade of aftershave and cologne bottles that tumbled to the floor, their sound almost musical as they rattled together on the thick carpet. A couple struck each other hard enough to break, and the scents instantly filled the air. Trillion cringed back, ducking partly behind the end of the dresser, the gun waving generally in the direction of the stranger. "Who…who are you?"

The stranger leaned in the doorway, his arms crossed over his chest, his casual stance indicating that seeing a rock star with a gun in his mouth was not at all unusual.

"I said who are you, and what do you want?" Trillion asked again, his voice hitching.

The stranger lifted his head and sniffed the air. "Aqua Velva, an oldie but goody." The man turned and strolled into the living room.

Trillion cowered in the corner, with the gun pointed at the doorway. His breath came in hitches, fear and the cloying scent from the broken bottles combining to make his stomach want to empty itself again. He listened, and after a few moments heard a familiar sound from the living room; the soft sound of an electric guitar being played without the benefit of an amplifier.

Clutching the dresser for support, Trillion wobbled to his feet, and with the gun thrust out before him, tip-toed around the broken glass to the bedroom door. He peeked around the doorframe like a child playing hide-and-seek. The stranger sat on the couch in front of the table that still held the mirror and bag of coke. He was leaned back, his legs crossed. He'd taken Trillion's Les Paul from where it hung on the wall by the fireplace and was playing it, his eyes half closed as though truly enjoying himself. He blew through some Van Halen riffs, some Stevie Ray Vaughan, and then some things Trillion had never heard before. Standing in the doorway, gun in hand and so scared that he wondered that he hadn't wet his pants, the startling thought that came to Trillion was; 'I thought I was good, but if I practiced for two hundred years I couldn't play like that.'

The stranger stopped playing and looked at Trillion. "Come on in, Chuck."

"Dave sent you, didn't he? You brought the recording. He told you to call me Chuck."

The stranger shook his head. "Nope."

"Then who are you and what do you want? And how did you know my real name?"

The stranger smiled. "You wouldn't believe me if I told you." He went back to playing, his fingers a blur.

Trillion crept into the room and circled the couch so he stood across the table from the stranger, the gun still aimed at the man. The stranger ignored him, apparently engrossed in his musical interests.

"I've got a gun pointed at you."

The stranger stopped playing and looked up, his head tipped slightly as many people do when puzzled.

"Why?"

"Why what?" Trillian quizzed, his voice trembling

The stranger laid the guitar in his lap and leaned forward slightly. "Why do you have a gun pointed at me?"

"To protect myself, I…I don't know who you are or what you want." Trillion stammered. "For all I know you might rob me, or kill me."

"So?"

"So!"

The stranger laid the guitar beside him on the couch. "Nice axe, but I personally prefer a Strat. You know if it's good enough for Clapton…" The stranger shrugged, put his hands on his knees and stood up. Trillion stepped back. The stranger crossed his arms over his chest again. "So what if I killed you? If I'm not mistaken you had a gun barrel in your mouth a few minutes ago. Was that because you like the taste of steel?"

"I….I…."

"Well put," the stranger said, a wry smile curling the corners of his mouth. He picked up the guitar, and crossing the room, hung it on the wall. "Funny how someone who thinks he's ready to die changes his mind when he feels the decision is no longer his. I'm going to get something to drink. You want something?" He nodded toward the kitchen.

Trillion shook his head numbly.

The stranger ambled into the kitchen, humming softly. Trillion recognized the tune. It was a ballad from his first album; a love song. He shuffled to the kitchen door and peeked in. The stranger was standing before the open refrigerator, looking in, with his hands in his pockets. He was about five-ten or eleven, fiftyish, with a beard and mustache. His hair was fairly long and threaded with gray as was his beard. He wore jeans and a long sleeved work shirt, blue and white checked, with the sleeves rolled up. He looked like a typical cab driver or construction worker.

The stranger pulled a bottle of orange juice from the fridge, spun off the cap and tossed it in the trashcan at the far end of the kitchen. He grinned at Trillion. "Two points. Sure you don't want something?"

"There wasn't any orange juice in there."

"Sure there was." The stranger smiled and walked back toward the living room. Trillion stepped back, keeping his distance. The man dropped back down on the couch. "Why don't you sit down?"

Trillion stood staring.

"Please." The man gestured toward a chair. Trillion eased into it, ready to run in a heartbeat.

"And how about the gun?" the man asked.

"I think I'll keep it." Trillian hated that he was whining, but was too scared to stop.

The man shrugged. "Suit yourself." He looked around. "Nice digs." He glanced at the bag of cocaine. "Think we could dispose of that. It bothers me."

"What are you, a goody two shoes?"

"I suppose you could say that."

"There's a thousand dollars' worth of stuff there."

The man's eyes narrowed, his expression showing impatience for the first time. "What's it matter to you? You eat a gun you won't need it."

"I'll keep it just the same."

The man nodded. "OK. That's what I'm all about, free will."

"OK mister free will. Now I want to know who you are."

The man rubbed his chin thoughtfully. "You know Thanksgiving is tomorrow? Nice holiday. Makes even the most jaded individuals realize how good they've got it." The man stared Trillion in the eyes. "Usually," he added.

"Save the lecture. You don't know a thing about me."

"Wrong, Chuck. I know everything about you. I know things you've forgotten and things you don't even know about yourself."

"Yeah, like what?"

"Sure you want to know?"

Trillion nodded uncertainly.

"I know that your father took off before you were born and that your mother died of cancer when you were nine. I know your grandmother raised you, and that she lives in Knoxville Tennessee in a mobile home that she bought with the pitiful insurance settlement she got after your grandfather was killed working in a stone quarry." The man paused for effect. Trillion stared, open-mouthed. The man continued, "I know that you send her a fat check each month and that she cashes them and deposits the cash in a savings account in both her name and yours; just in case your career falls flat. She watches TV enough to know that such things happen. I know that she bought you your first guitar, an old Fender acoustic, with money that she borrowed by pawning her engagement ring."

The man leaned forward. "I also know that an occasional visit from you would mean more to her than all the checks you could ever possibly send." The man sipped his juice. "Oh, yeah," he added. I also know that you're twenty four years, three months, nine days and four minutes old; the seconds change too quickly to bother mentioning. And that when you're forty-eight you'll have the same kind of cancer that killed your mother." He leaned back and sipped his juice. "But I wouldn't worry about that too much. Between now and then they'll make great strides in treating cancer. Besides, you plan on killing yourself anyway."

The man sipped his juice calmly. Fear and confusion getting the best of him, Trillion's eyes rolled back and he slid out of his chair and landed in a heap on the floor.

Stave 3

He opened his eyes. The man was at the huge home entertainment center glancing through the long row of CDs. With a colossal effort, Trillion struggled to his feet. The man looked around and smiled. "Hi. Your gun's on the table there."

Trillion shook his head and looked around the room. Everything was where it belonged and the revolver was on the coffee table by the bag of cocaine. His head was beginning to clear, either from the coke wearing off or from the stress of the situation, or a little of both. At least he knew that this guy didn't plan on killing him. If he did he'd missed a golden opportunity while Trillion was in a heap on the floor.

"You know, that really does bother me." The man pointed at the bag of cocaine and it disappeared, like a special effect from a movie.

"How'd you do that?"

"Don't worry, it's in the kitchen. I told you I'm all about free will. It'll be there if you want it later. I just didn't want to keep looking at it."

"How'd you do that?" Trillion asked again.

The man pointed toward the rocking chair Trillion had fallen from. The chair began to rock, gently, invitingly. "You look like you need to sit down." His legs like rubber bands, Trillion dropped in the chair.

"Better?"

Trillion shook his head. The man smiled and sat down on the couch again. "I don't know if you're ready for this but I'm a busy man. You ever watch movies?"

"What?"

"Movies; you know, moving pictures on TV or in the theatre." Trillion just stared at him.

"Okay, let's cut to the chase. Have you ever seen "It's A Wonderful Life"?

"The ghost of Christmas past, that one?" Trillian asked uncertainly.

The man shook his head. "Wrong movie, right idea, sort of. You know, Jimmy Stewart as George Bailey. Bedford Falls, Clarence the Angel. Any bells going off?"

"Yeah, I remember." Trillion's eyes widened. "No way, you're telling me you're my guardian angel. Get real. I'm not that stoned! No way!" His voice came out all stutter and panic

"Way. But not exactly." The man stood and walked around the room, his hands clasped behind his back. "Fact is I'm God."

"You're a psycho, and I'm calling the law." Trillion jumped up and reached for the phone on the end table, then realizing that he'd heaved it at the TV after Dave's call, turned and stumbled through the kitchen door. As he reached for the wall phone, it disappeared, just as the bag of coke had. Trillion felt dizzy and clutched the doorframe.

His head cleared after a moment and he slowly walked back into the living room. The man sat on the couch, twiddling his thumbs.

"This isn't funny," Trillion whispered.

"I'm not trying to be funny," God said. "I'm deadly serious. I'm always serious. I'm here because you're planning to commit suicide."

"And you're here to change my mind? To show me what a wonderful life I've had?"

"No."

"No?"

God leaned forward. "Chuck, I'm going to be square with you. I always am. I didn't write those movies, you know. I was just a character in them. But that's Okay. They were good stories and I've always thought that I'd have handled the situations that way. Plus there was a logic to them; a reason for the hero to be helped. Scrooge was an evil man but he had one friend, Jacob Marley, who cared about him enough to go to bat for him. And trust Me; his chances weren't great from the start, and I know about these things. George Bailey was a good man hit by a lot of bad luck. His only fault was that he fell head first into a well of self-pity, convinced that the world and those living on it would be better off without him. But he deserved to be shown how important he'd been to so many people. How many people's lives he'd changed for the better. And how many people's lives he might change in the future. But the sad fact is in your case those things just don't apply."

Are you really God," Chuck asked softly, his voice trembling. "Really?"

God nodded.

"But you're not here to stop me from killing myself?"

God shook His head.

"Why…why not?"

"Chuck," God said softly, calmly, "It saddens me to say it, but other than your grandmother, who loves you like you were her own child, I can't for the life of me think of anyone who would suffer for your death, or anyone who would benefit from your living. And your grandmother spends most of her waking hours worrying herself sick about you. For some reason she feels she failed you. She knows you are miserable; she picks it up from your voice when you get around to calling her every year or so. And she can see it on your face when she sees you on TV. She worries that you're losing weight; that you're not eating right, that you're not getting enough rest. She worries about you doing drugs, but that's a worry she hides inside. Tries to hide it even from herself."

"How do you know all this?" Chuck interrupted.

God rolled His eyes. "Come on Chuck."

"So you're saying that it'd be no great loss if I killed myself, but then you say how much my grandmother cares about me. What about her? Huh? What about her?" Chuck's voice had gained a hint of desperation. "She'd care!"

"Yes, she would. She would be hurt. But after a while she wouldn't hurt so much. And a while later she'd realize she wasn't at fault. And though she'd miss you, and she'd be sorry you were gone; she'd eventually be at peace with the fact. And temporary hurt is better than constant hurt."

"How can you be so sure she'd be at peace?"

God smiled. "I'd see to it."

Stave 4

Chuck looked at his feet. "You can do that? Make somebody be at peace?"

"Yeah, I can."

Chuck looked up, his eyes narrow. "Why didn't you ever do that for me?" he growled.

"Why didn't you ask?"

Chuck's eyes found his feet again. "Have I really been that bad? What have I done that makes me such a hopeless case?"

"Watch." God stood and crossed the room. He had a disc in his hand. He slid it into the DVD player atop the TV, pushed the play button and a picture appeared on the spider-webbed screen. The MTV logo flashed on, the image disjointed behind the fractured glass. The picture flickered and a wisp of acrid smoke curled from air slots on top of the set.

"I thought you said you didn't have the disc."

"No," God said. "I said Dave didn't send me over with it. Watch." It wasn't said like a request.

"Welcome back to our exclusive interview with Trillion Kane," a pretty brunette said. "Trillion joined us this evening to talk about his upcoming album, but before the break he began baring his soul, so to speak. Trillion, you were saying?"

Chuck's face filled the screen, fractured as if seen through a kaleidoscope. The eyes of the image on the screen were glazed and watery. He wobbled in his seat as he stared into the camera's lens. When he spoke his voice was thick, his speech slurred.

'I said that life sucks, didn't I? Yeah…that's it. I said when you hit the top everybody wants a piece of you." Chuck turned from the camera, confused and searching. "Where…Huh…Oh yeah." He'd lost track of which camera was on. 'Yeah, OK."

He faced front again. "My life's not worth living. There's not a day that I don't think about ending it, and anybody out there with any sense oughta' think about it too.' The Chuck on the TV wobbled, nearly falling from his chair. The pretty brunette reached to help but he shrugged her off. "Lemme go!" He stood up and walked from the scene, cursing and muttering as he went, the network's sensor replacing words with silence where necessary.

God hit the stop button. "That's the worst of it: your crescendo; the finale. You started off well enough, talking about the album and a possible tour, but it was obvious from the start you were wasted. Then you started getting cranked up, whining and complaining, talking about how bad your life is. That went on during the break and the director almost didn't put you back on afterwards. But he did. Of course he couldn't have guessed that one of the world's biggest rock stars would look into the camera and tell millions of people that suicide was a fine and dandy option. That a person who has more than most of them could ever dream of having has nothing to live for." God walked to the large window that looked down on the street twelve stories below. He looked out, his back to Chuck, his hands in his pockets.

"How many people," He continued solemnly, "How many people who saw that will buy into your foolish ravings? How many people who've lost a loved one and feel alone? How many people who've been laid off and don't know how they'll feed their families? How many teenagers who think their life's over because their boyfriend or girlfriend dumped them? How many seventy-five pound girls who look in the mirror and think they're social outcasts because they don't weigh seventy pounds?"

God turned and looked at Chuck. Chuck looked up at Him, his eyes watery and his chin quivering. "How many people," God continued, "people with a great deal to live for will end their lives because you told them it was the right thing to do?"

Stave 5

Chuck hung his head, his hands covering his face. He felt like crying but did his best to hold it back, afraid that if he started he might never stop.

"Come here", God said firmly.

Chuck didn't move.

"Come here Chuck, now! I have something to show you."

Chuck stood and shuffled to the window. God held back the drape and pointed down the street. "See that guy, the one in front of the department store in the Santa Clause suit greeting people?" Chuck peered through the frosty window. It had gotten really cold since the sun went down.

God pointed. "That man is one of the finest keyboard players in the state. Incredible talent, but he's out of work. The band he was in fell apart. Everybody in the band, everybody but him that is, was more interested in their next fix than in their next gig. So here's this killer keyboard man, out of work with a wife and two kids. Tough times, right? So what's he do? Sit and cry? Kill himself? No! He gets a job playing Santa Clause. It ain't the Palace kid, but you're workin', right? The guy's got a lot of reasons to give up, but he finds reasons to keep going. He does what's necessary."

"Maybe he's got more reasons to live than I do," Chuck whispered.

God sniffed. "Everybody's got reasons. You've just got to be smart enough to realize it." God let the drape fall closed and walked to the coffee table.

"I've got to take off, Chuck, so let's get down to brass tacks."

"What? If you didn't come to save me, what are you here for?"

"That." God pointed toward the coffee table. Where the bag of coke had been when this whole nightmare started there was now a manila envelope. It wasn't very thick but there was clearly something in it.

"What is it?" Chuck backed up, afraid to be too close to the envelope.

"What are you worth, Chuck? In dollars I mean?"

"I don't know. A lot I guess."

"Well I know. As of this minute your net worth is forty-nine million, three hundred eighty-three thousand and nine dollars, and seventeen cents." He paused for a beat,. "eighteen cents,..nineteen…twenty. And if you kill yourself, all of that money will be tied up in lawsuits for the next five years while the record company and publishing company and the lawyers all grab for their piece of the pie. All but Dave, that is. He's that most rare of all species, an honest agent. All he wants is what he's earned. You're lucky to have him as an agent, and friend."

Chuck closed his eyes. "Yeah, I know." It came out a hoarse whisper.

"So," God continued, "What I want you to do is look over the papers in yon envelope." He swept his hand toward the table. "It's a copy of your will, with a few changes. It leaves your grandmother enough to live quite comfortably for the rest of her life. And knowing her as I do, I'm sure that's all she would accept. The balance will be put in a trust, under Dave's control, to be divided among worthy charities of his choosing and at his discretion. Before you do anything rash, I would like for you to read it and sign it."

"You would like for me to? I don't have to?"

"Nope, like I said, I'm all about free will. You can do as you please once I'm gone, but since you didn't bother doing much good on the way up, it's a chance to at least do something good on the way out."

Chuck looked at his hands, turning them over like he'd never seen them before. After a few seconds he dug the nail of his right thumb into the back of his left hand till blood began to ooze from the crescent shaped wound. He winced at the pain. He looked at God.

"This isn't a dream is it? I'm not going to wake up and realize it was all in my head?"

"No Chuck, it's for real." God shoved His hands in the pockets of His jeans. "Gotta' go." He nodded at the table. "There's the will, there's the gun, the coke's on the kitchen counter. It's up to you, my man. Free will. That's what it's all about." He strolled to the apartment's front door, turning before leaving. "It's up to you to do what's right, or what's wrong. Free will, man! Ain't it a great thing?" God glanced at His wrist. "Hey, it's past midnight, Happy Thanksgiving Chuck!"

He turned and walked out the door, without bothering to open it first.

Stave 6

Chuck stood where he was, trembling in his alligator boots. When he felt he could take a step without crumbling, he walked to the DVD player. He pushed the power button, then the eject button. The disc popped out; the disk that Dave didn't send. He left it hanging in the machine, afraid to touch it.

He looked at the table, the envelope and the revolver just inches apart. By leaning just a little he could see the bag of cocaine on the kitchen counter. He stared hard at it for a long time, till his vision began to double. When he finally moved, he walked into the kitchen. He leaned on the counter for a while, then, his hands shaking badly, picked up the bag of cocaine. Sniffling reflexively, he turned on the hot water, stuffed the bag down the garbage disposal and flipped on the switch. A muffled grinding noise came from the drain and a small white cloud rose into the air. Chuck ignored it and walked to where the wall phone now hung again in its usual place. He picked up the receiver and punched some numbers. "Hello," Dave answered after the fourth ring.

"Dave, it's Tril…. it's Chuck."

"What is it, Chuck?" Dave asked warily.

"I…I've got some things I need your help on, Dave. I really need you. It shouldn't take too long to do it, a week maybe, but I really need you. After that you can quit me if you want and I wouldn't blame you a bit. They're things I'd do myself, but I'd probably screw them up. Plus I've got a date soon and I don't know how long I'll be gone."

"A date? With who?"

"Betty Ford."

"Are you OK Chuck?"

"I don't know. Maybe not, but I think I might be."

"What is it you want me to do?"

"Just a few things, but I'm sure the more I think about it the more I'll come up with. But the most important thing, the absolute most important thing is to hit the phones first thing in the morning! Call MTV, VH1, the Today Show, everybody! Everybody you can think of. I need airtime as soon as possible. I've done a lot of damage and I want to undo as much of it as possible. It might be too late, but I have to try. I have to. That's the most urgent thing. Then I want you to do some research. Find some people who need help; financial help. I don't care if it's a family who has medical bills they can't pay or a major charity. Just as long as it's a worthy cause and it's legit. I trust you Dave. You'll choose wisely. We're going to start sharing the wealth." Chuck was surprised to find he was smiling. "After all, you can't take it with you, right?"

"Right." Dave paused. "Are you sure you're OK Chuck, really?"

"I think so Dave. Listen, I've gotta' go. I have another call to make. You get started first thing in the AM. We'll talk more tomorrow, OK? And Dave, happy Thanksgiving."

"You too, Chuck." Dave hung up.

Chuck held down the phone hook till he got a dial tone. He dialed a longer number this time, and it took eleven rings for an old, drowsy voice to say hello.

"Grandma, it's me, Chuck. I'm sorry to call so late, but I've got a lot to tell you. I mostly called to tell you happy Thanksgiving, and that I love you."

Epilogue

A man exited the door of the department store, waved at the security guard who locked the door behind him and turned to walk to the bus stop. It had been a very long day, the store open till midnight because of the holiday tomorrow. He pulled his coat collar up and started to walk, the growing wind slapping the coat tail against his legs in rhythm with his strides. He'd taken only a few steps when a man appeared in front of him; a man with graying hair and dressed in jeans and a blue and white checked shirt. The man wore no coat, but though he had his hands in his pockets he didn't appear to be bothered by the night's chill.

"Aren't you the one who plays Santa Clause here?" the man asked.

"Yeah, why?" the off-duty Santa asked cautiously.

"Store's closed tomorrow, right?" the stranger in the checked shirt asked.

"Yeah, it's Thanksgiving."

"I know. But you'll be here the next day, right."

"Are you kidding? The day after Thanksgiving's Black Friday, the busiest shopping day of the year. I'll be here. Why?"

The stranger glanced toward the upper levels of the high-rise apartment building across the street. He then again looked at the off-duty Santa. "Friday morning a man named Dave is going to walk up to you and offer you a job playing keyboards for Trillion Kane. He's not crazy, and it'd be a good idea to listen to what he has to say."

"Are you serious? How do you know that?" The stranger in the checked shirt just shrugged, smiled and started to turn away.

"Wait, please! Do I know you?"

"I sure hope so. Happy Thanksgiving!" The man walked off down the street, whistling a Christmas song.

The End

AN UNSELFISH WISH

Jeremiah Yoder and his four-year old son Noah stood side by side in ankle-deep mud, which was covered first by a layer of slush and then an uneven crust of ice. It was the underlying mud, created by more than a week of continuous rainfall before the snow and sleet, all topped by a surprising warm spell that had caused their troubles. The pair would look odd to most people driving by on the two-lane rural Pennsylvania road. A big man in high, well-used work boots and black pants of coarse cloth, Jeremiah's dark blue work shirt was buttoned up to the collar, and he wore a broad brimmed hat with a black crown and a dark brown brim. Jeremiah stood like a statue, his feet apart, and his arms behind him, his hands uncharacteristically clenched in fists. Noah stood beside him, posed identically, and dressed identically, the top of his hat barely reaching his father's belt; his hands also clenched in small fists behind him. Jeremiah's fists were clenched not in anger, but in frustration, an emotion people of his heritage found shameful. Little Noah's fists were clenched because his fathers were. Most people driving by who had seen any of the 'Austin Powers' movies wouldn't be able to not think 'mini-me' at the sight of Noah, but the idea would never occur to Jeremiah; the Amish don't go to movies.

At the sound of the garage door rattling closed, Josh Prather shot through the house like a small missile, or more exactly, like a four-year old boy who just heard his father come home as the sun was beginning to set on the day two days before Christmas. It seemed to be getting darker earlier every day; something a young boy pays attention to as Christmas draws near.

James Prather wiped his feet on the hemp mat at the back door before stepping into the kitchen. Josh tackled him around his knees before he'd taken his second step, as he hung his jacket on the rack by the door. "Hi Daddy Merry Christmas!"

James made a show of trying to shake loose of the weight anchoring him to the spot. "Hey Buddy, Christmas isn't for two days, you know."

Josh's mother Betty stepped up next to her husband and put her arm around his waist. "Don't you remember when you were four?"

"No, as a matter of fact, I don't. Thank you so much for reminding me." Then, the playfulness gone from his voice, James said, "Did you see Jeremiah's shop?"

"Just that something doesn't look right. What's happened?"

The Prathers lived adjacent to Jeremiah and Sarah Yoder's small farm. They had felt no insignificant amount of hesitance when considering moving into an area mostly dotted with Amish farms and homesteads. As it turned out, they couldn't have wished for better neighbors than the Yoders; the very nature of their lifestyle making them the perfect family with whom to share a property line. Much of the other property around the Yoder farm was empty; many of the older, most traditional Amish families choosing to move on as modern growth encroached on the area. Part of the area's charm slowly drifted away as the number of black buggies on the rural roads dwindled perceptibly.

"It's the mud." James answered. "It slid."

"What slid?"

"His shop; the whole building slid. The whole thing is made of logs. It must weigh a ton: maybe two. It sits on two long split logs. It might as well be on skis. I'm sure nobody gave it a thought when his father built the place. Back then there were still woods where a lot of land has been clear cut for housing developments. The tree roots kept the soil in place. Now when it rains hard and the runoff comes down off the hills it rolls mud right across his fields. Then you add a sixty mile an hour wind off the mountain pushing on it; it's just too much. You can't really tell it from here, but if it slides another twenty-five feet or so, it'll go over the bank and drop right into the road."

"Oh No!" Betty immediately grasped the gravity of the situation. Through no fault of his own,

Jeramiah had fallen on hard times, as had many of the small farmers in the area; Amish, and others alike. A combination of several years of bad weather and just plain bad luck had nearly brought his farming to a halt. His father suffered a heart attack and was no longer able to help him. A drought dried up his well, and since he wouldn't consider using a well driller, hand digging one took almost a week away from the farm. James had offered to loan Jeremiah the money for a driller if he wanted to use one. He didn't try to pressure him, only offered. Jeremiah shook his hand and said, "Thank you James, but no." James helped him dig the well. And Bess; his only horse; the one the song 'The old gray Mare' must have been written about was barely able to pull a plow any longer.

So Jeramiah supported his family by building furniture. His furniture was beautifully fashioned; the work of an artisan who truly cared about his craft. He'd struck deals with some of the area merchants, his largest customer being Murphy's Hardware. They displayed his furniture on their long front porch. Some of the smaller grocery stores kept a few of his rocking chairs and cradles in their front windows. And one of the area Amish markets carried his furniture in the spring and summer.

Every stick of Jeramiah's furniture was crafted with hand tools and one lathe powered by a foot treadle like an old sewing machine. Most of his tools were handed down; some were purchased new: but all were in the log shed that hung precariously close to taking a long drop to a very hard stop.

So, Both James and Betty grasped the severity of Jeramiah's problem. If his shop was gone, so was his only income.

James headed for the back door, grabbing his jacket from where he'd hung it only minutes ago.

Josh saw his dad rushing toward the door and ran to his mother. "Mommy, "Where's Daddy going?"

When Betty didn't answer immediately, he asked again, louder, and more insistently, "Where's Daddy going, Mommy? He's just about running. Is something wrong? I saw you two looking out the window toward Noah's house. Is something wrong over there?"

Surprisingly, despite lifestyles that couldn't be more different if they were from different planets, Josh and Noah had gravitated to each other and become fast friends. It seems the things that are the same about all four-year old boys outweigh the differences. During the school year Josh went to Noah's nearly every evening, and almost always came home with a new and interesting tidbit of information about Amish life.

During summer break, Noah loved to come over and help with Betty's flower garden. The boy had a green thumb.

James stopped before going out the door and pulled on boots. He looked back. "Put your boots on Josh, we're going next door."

Betty said, "James," her eyebrows raised questioningly.

"It's his best friend."

Josh looked to his mother, who nodded. "Okay. I'll keep dinner warm. Then as her two men went out the door she added, "You two be careful."

James gave her a thumbs-up and said, "Will do." Josh gave her an identical thumbs-up and said, "Will do."

Betty thought, 'That's some mini-me you've got there.'

The digital clock on the range said ten minutes till ten when Betty finally saw James walk into the zone of light thrown by the floodlights that covered their yard on the side of the house facing the Yoder farm. Before he was close to the house she could see he was covered with mud nearly to his waist. Then she saw he was carrying something. At first she couldn't tell what. When he was close enough that she could tell it was Josh he was carrying, she dropped the cup of lukewarm coffee she'd been nursing for nearly an hour and ran from the door, faster than she ever would have thought she could run, crying harder than she ever thought she could cry. When she reached James, she threw her arms around both of them and sobbed till she lost her breath. Then Josh said, "Why are you crying Mommy?" He was uninjured, just mud covered and sound asleep.

"He's okay, hon," James said, the exhaustion clear in his voice.

"How about you?"

"Me, too," he said tiredly.

Betty nodded toward the darkness in the direction of the Yoder's. "What's it look like?"

"Not good. He readjusted his hold on Josh and said, "Let's hose him off and put him in bed, then I'll tell you about it, okay?"

'You want me to take him?"

"No, I'm already filthy, I'll take him in."

"Okay, I'll start coffee."

Twenty minutes later Betty and James sat at the kitchen table. Josh was clean, dry, and under the covers. James had showered and was bundled up in a ski jacket, sipping his second cup of coffee, still trying to get warm. It wasn't super cold out, not for Pennsylvania on the 23rd of December, but plenty cold enough for working outside on a damp night.

James told her the situation next door. "We did about all we could do with it getting dark. That building's not going to be stable again till it's pulled back away from the bank to more solid ground. Then when the ground dries, it can be jacked up and stone put under it."

"But you said it weighs a ton. How can he pull it up?"

"There's the problem. Most people would call a contractor, or at least a farmer with a tractor to pull it up. But Jeramiah won't do that."

"I don't understand. Why do they have to be so stubborn? Are they too proud to accept help? Why no tractors? Why no electricity? How did you even see to work over there?" Betty sounded irritated

Sarah brought out some oil lamps. It was enough for what we could do, which wasn't much."

"What did you do?"

Before answering Betty's question, James said, "Jeremiah's not stubborn, or proud. He's living what he was taught and what he believes. Isn't that what you would want Josh to do?"

He watched for the calm in her eyes, and when he saw it, he went on. "There's a Bible verse; I wouldn't know where to find it, but it says not to be conformed to the world. The Amish really take it seriously. They feel that easy access to electricity and cars and could open up too many temptations.

"How do you know so much?"

"The internet; I figured if I was going to be a good neighbor, I better have my ducks in a row. So I did a little studying."

"I know stuff, too." They looked around and found Josh was standing in the hallway door, his eyes blurry with sleep.

James winked at him. "Yeah, what stuff do you know, buddy?"

Josh got a terribly serious look of sadness on his face. "Noah doesn't believe in Santa Claus."

Betty said, "No Santa? Well that's a real shame. Come here." She patted her knee.

Josh climbed on her lap. At four, he considered himself almost grown up. But on her lap he was still her baby. "Why don't you go back to bed hon? And in the morning when we're all really awake you can tell us more, okay."

James said, "We'll go back over to Noah's tomorrow and look things over. How's that?"

"Kay." Josh padded off down the hall, and they heard his door close.

James gulped half a cup of coffee the temperature and color of the bath water he'd sent down the drain just a little while before, and said, "Well, as soon as I got there I called Frank Murphy down at Murphy's Hardware. He called in his brother, and a couple of his guys that were off, and they came out with some tools and big logging ropes. About all we could do tonight was split some of Jeremiah's firewood into big stakes and drive them in as deep as we could on both sides of the building. Then we tied six ropes around the building from one side to the other; one a couple feet off the ground and then worked our way up as high as we could reach. So the building's slung there like it's in a big…"

"""Bra"

James smiled, despite his weariness. "Actually, I was thinking, net.

"Will it hold? Will it keep it from falling?"

"I hope so, at least long enough to figure something out. But I still don't

70

know how he'll get it pulled back up.

"Horses, maybe?"

"James shook his head. "Don't know. Bess is on her last legs, literally; and she's just an average size plow horse. She looks huge to you or me if we stand beside her, but Frank said she couldn't have pulled it off ten years ago. He's an old farm guy, and he thinks it would take a big draft horse, maybe two, if not more. I mean the big ones; Clydesdale size. Like the giants in the Budweiser commercials." They wouldn't need that kind of pedigree, just that kind of power. James stared into his empty coffee cup and shook his head slowly.

"Is there somebody? Can you find somebody with big horses?"

"I don't know; I'm not really up on that kind of thing. Frank might be able to find somebody. But close enough to get them here before the building goes over the edge, and at Christmas. I just don't know.

Oh, I have to ask. Josh came home as dirty as you. What was he doing?"

"He was helping. He and Noah made sure we had plenty of water to drink. They moved the lamps to where we needed them. And more than once he wiped the mud from our eyes. Not just mine but everybody's. He really cares. I think we done good," James said in a rare display of rural jargon.

So what do you have in mind tomorrow?"

Get ready. We'll wheelbarrow in a bunch of big stones so they'll be there when we get Jeremiah's shop back where it belongs."

"Well, listen to you; Mister glass-half-full all of the sudden."

"Maybe it's just the Christmas spirit." James smiled over the coffee stained rim of his cup, and then set it down perfectly on the ring it had made on the kitchen table. "I'm tired."

"Go to bed. You elves are going to have a tough Christmas Eve. I watched a little of the news. I had to do something besides stare out that window. They said we might get some sleet or maybe even snow overnight and into tomorrow, and a lot of wind."

James stood up. "I'm going to bed before my glass starts to look half empty."

"I'll be in in a little while."

"Got some more worrying to do first, huh?"

Josh was the first one up the next morning. Before six am he shouted from his room, "Mommy, Daddy!" Scared, both parents rushed to his room. Betty got to him first. "What, Honey? What's wrong?"

 Rubbing his eyes, he asked, Did Santa come?"

"No, Honey. It's not Christmas yet. It's Christmas Eve. Christmas is tomorrow."

"Good," Josh said, his face set and serious. "We have to go to the hardware store."

"Why? James asked.

"I have to see Santa. I have to ask him for something."

Betty said, "Hon, you saw Santa day-before-yesterday. Remember? You sat on his lap and told him what you want."

With a look of determination that should have looked comical on the face of a four-year old, but didn't, Josh said, "I have to talk to him. There's something else. It's important. Can we go? Will you take me?"

"I thought you were going to go help Daddy at Noah's house."

I'll go over when we get back from the store, okay. I have to talk to him."

Betty saw how determined he was. "All right, but it's not even six yet. They don't open till nine. It'll have to wait till then. You go ahead and get dressed, and dress warm. It was supposed to get pretty cold overnight, and I don't think it's warmed up much yet."

Josh leapt from his bed and started getting dressed at a remarkable pace.

James said, "Take it easy, boy. Santa won't be there till nine. Christmas Eve is a busy day for him. Give him a break, okay."

Josh nodded, and went on dressing at a more leisurely pace.

"That's better. Get dressed, brush your teeth, then come on in the kitchen and get some oatmeal." "Workingman's food," James added, when Josh cringed.

Betty glanced out the window over the sink before setting a skillet on the range and turning on the burner. For the hundredth time in the last two days she thought of Sarah Yoder fixing breakfast on a wood stove next door, and wondered how she could do it. Unbelievable devotion to her beliefs; enviable devotion, in fact.

 Then the morning sun glinted off the expanse of white. "Oh, wow." She said.

"What?"

"Snow," She answered,"Two inches, easy. Icy on top; looks like you could skate on it."

James peered over her shoulder. "That's not going to make working next door any easier."

"Really, Captain Obvious? What can you do anyway?"

"Try to drive some big wedges under the downhill end of it, like putting chocks under a truck's tires. And we talked about clearing away the snow and slush uphill, so when we do find a way to pull it up the way will be clearer."

"There's that glass-half full guy I love again."

James looked out the window. It might be a necessary tool today. They heard the throb of a big engine behind their house. "There's Frank and his guys; gotta' roll." As he went out the door he said, you'll manage to sit close by when Josh talks to Santa, right."

"I always do. I'll keep an ear open. You be careful."

James blew a kiss her way and they went toward their separate Christmas Eve missions; he to the aid of a neighbor, she to prepare for a visit to Santa that seemed to be of amazing importance to her four-year old.

Then the unimaginable happened; James called from next door; on his cell phone of course, with the news that because of the snow and ice Frank had decided not to open the hardware store that day. Santa would not be available for Christmas Eve visits. Frank would still respond to emergency calls forwarded to his cell phone; burst pipes, furnaces out of commission and the like. Last minute Santa Clause visits unfortunately didn't make the cut.

James came home just before noon for a change of clothes and to pick up a thermos of hot coffee. Betty had a bowl of soup and a grilled cheese waiting; a quick but nourishing fill-up for his battle with the elements. He had little to report; beyond the fact that the temperature was dropping and the wind was picking up, coming in strong gusts against the big slab-sided wall of Jeremiah's shop; threatening to push it closer to the edge of the drop. Their efforts to stop its slide had so far been successful, but nobody was very confident of the long term. Frank had strongly urged Jeremiah to let him bring his backhoe in to pull the building back into place. Jeremiah had respectfully declined the offer and gone on working like a machine. James looked in the living room and saw Josh sitting by the Christmas tree crying silently. He asked, "You okay, Pal?"

Josh answered, "Noah doesn't believe in Santa Clause."

James walked over and put his hand on his son's head and asked, "Do you want to go over to Noah's house and help? Then, "We could really use you. We'll talk about it with Mommy when we come home. We'll be home before dark. It is Christmas Eve, you know.

"Yeah." Josh bundled up, and holding his father's hand, walked across the ice-crusted snow to the Prather's, to resume the project of rescuing Jeremiah's furniture shop.

When the winter sun was low on the western horizon, the men, women and children working were forced by the oncoming darkness and worsening weather to stop for the night.

Bathed, and with teeth brushed, Josh sat on his bed in Star Wars pajamas he'd outgrow in less than another year.

His parents sat with him. James asked, "Okay boy, what did you want to add to your Christmas list so bad that you almost dragged your mom down to Murphy's over a sheet of ice? I told you, you're too young for an X-box, even if Santa is on your side." He looked at Betty.

"No, it's something important." Josh insisted.

"Yeah, like what?"

"It doesn't matter. It's too late. I didn't get to ask him." He was near tears.

Betty put her arm around him. "Take it easy, honey. You know what?"

"What?"

"Santa's always listening. Like the song says; he knows if you've been bad or good, so be good for goodness sake. If he knows all that; he must know what you want; even if you didn't get to tell him in person.

"You think so?"

"James said, "Especially if it's as important as you said."

Betty said, "My grandmother used to say, "God hears every prayer, but He's

a little bit disappointed by the selfish ones. Maybe Santa is the same way. You think hard about what you want, and you might be surprised, especially if it's not something selfish.

"Kind of like a wish?"

"Yeah, like a wish."

James asked, "You want to tell us what it is?"

"Nope."

"Okay." He pulled the blanket up to Josh's chin. "You go to sleep. Tomorrow's Christmas. You don't want to sleep through it, do you?"

James and Betty sat in the living room for a while, talking. Betty asked about Jeremiah's shop.

James said, "Frank's still trying to find someone with big horses. So far, no luck. There's one man about twenty miles south of here he hasn't heard back from yet so there's still a chance. I hope he hears from him soon. I think Jeremiah's building is living on borrowed time. I wish there was something more we could do."

Betty put her hand on his. "There's definitely nothing more you can do tonight. You need to get some sleep. You're all thought out. Tomorrow's Christmas. You don't want to sleep through it, do you?"

James stood up. "No. I wonder what Josh wanted to ask Santa for so bad."

"I don't know, but he won't tell us. He's afraid if he does it'll be like a wish and telling will spoil it.

"Well we won't know now till tomorrow."

The next morning; Christmas morning, dawned crystal clear but cut by a biting wind. As James slowly came awake he heard the sound of the previous day's snow blowing against the windows; frozen into hard crystals by the nights plummeting temperatures. He just registered the shine of the early morning sun through the windows before the phone rang. Betty gave a little yelp beside him and grabbed at the phone and looked at the clock at the same time. Five-fifty-five; too early for panic, especially on Christmas morning. She put the phone to her ear, but hadn't had time to say hello, and James asked, "Who is it? What's wrong?"

She held up her index finger to silence him, and then hit the speaker button, and said hello.

Frank Murphy answered, his always growly voice blurred further by the rattling wind, "Betty, it's Frank. Is James outa' the rack yet?"

"Right here Frank. What's the big deal? The missus find about Jennie down at the Moose?"

Frank laughed aloud, unfazed. "You never miss a chance to be funny, even on Christmas morning do you? Betty, you do know he's just joking don't you?

"Yeah, Frank, I know."

"No, I'm a fool for all seasons," James said, loud enough for Frank to hear. "By the way; Merry Christmas."

"Right back atcha', Hey you gotta' see this!"

"See what? Where are you?"

"Right next door. Didn't you see my truck behind your house?"

"No, I didn't make it outa' bed yet.

"Well get your behind in gear and get over here. You gotta see this!"

"Yeah, you said that. See what?"

"You gotta see this! Come on!"

Betty, who had heard the whole thing asked, "What's going on?"

Jumping from bed, James rubbed the sleep from his eyes and pulled on jeans, then a shirt and socks and boots, "I don't know, but I think he wants me to see it."

Barefoot, and in pajamas, Betty followed him to the kitchen. James shrugged into his heavy work coat, and as he pulled on canvas gloves, looked out the window, across the snow covered land at the endangered building. It was still not in its normal place, but seemed out of sync from where his brain expected it to be. He splashed some water in his eyes, blotted them dry again, and then put on his glasses. In the dim morning light, when everything was barely more than shadows, things looked clearer, but still not right; or more correctly, too right, righter than they'd looked for days.

Before James was halfway to Jeremiah's building he saw Frank waving him on frantically, pointing a flashlight at the ground. When still twenty yards away he saw what Frank was so excited about. While still not where it originally sat, the building was a good forty feet farther from the edge of the embankment than it had been. The stakes they'd driven in the ground were still there, but the ropes hung limp. "What happened?" It was all he could manage to say.

"I Don't know. It's the way I found it when I got here."

"Where's Jeremiah? Does he know what happened?"

"He's in the house praying." Frank answered in a reverent whisper. I can't say as I blame him. But you haven't seen the strangest part yet."

"Stranger than a moving building?"

Frank pointed with his light toward where the building had originally set before the bad weather issues had conspired to endanger it. They followed the beam.

The frozen soil was chewed up in a path from the building toward its original location. Frank followed the damaged soil. James walked along. "Have you ever hunted, James?"

"Not since I was in my teens, why?"

Frank hunkered down like an Indian scout in an old western movie and pointed at the ground. "What are those?"

James followed his pointed finger. Hoof prints?"

Frank nodded. "Yeah."

"Horses?"

"Not a chance."

"How do you know?"

"Do you see any sign of shoes?"

James shook his head, and then realized the motion would be invisible in the dawn gloom. No."

"And…"

"And what?"

"The hooves are split. Do you know what that means?" Frank paused to let his question sink in.

Finally James said, "Deer?"

Frank said, "Yeah, deer. And I don't mean the white-tail deer you see thick as flies in the summer around here. I mean bigger deer than I've ever seen; at least six or maybe eight of them. And it looks for all the world like they were walking along side by side just as pretty as you please. James, I swear I didn't touch a drop of eggnog last night. You know I wouldn't when I knew I would be driving up here this morning, but I swear a hitch of deer pulled that building away from the edge of that drop during the night.

Betty handed James a cup of coffee as he came in the door. He took a sip and sat down at the kitchen table. As he bent over to unlace his boots he asked, "Josh isn't up yet? I thought sure he'd be out of bed by now."

"No. Not yet. I kind of wish he would get up. I was hoping he could enlighten us on how the Yoders celebrate Christmas. I know we see a few buggies pull up each year, and Sarah once told me they have family visit, but beyond that all we know is that Noah doesn't believe in Santa. And I'd really like to know what was so important that he needed to ask Santa for. He had plenty of things under the tree. Since we couldn't make that last visit we may never know what he wanted to ask for so bad. I just hope it wasn't something selfish."

"I'm almost certain it wasn't. Merry Christmas Hon."

The end

PROOF POSITIVE

"You're not really flying to Wisconsin on New year's eve, are you?" Wendy Janes asked Phillip Stotler as he zipped up his ski jacket and snugged the Velcro tight on the collar.

"Yep." Philip gave his scarf another wrap around his throat and nodded as best he could. "I hope I can get a cab." The wind whistled outside and snow pelted the windows.

"I haven't visited my aunt and uncle in three years. They really wanted me to make it for Christmas but I was too busy. So I'm going to make it one way or another. I also want to give Uncle Phil the results on that piece of <u>stuff</u> he sent me."

"They were odd."

"Odd's not the right word."

"This is the aunt and uncle you lived with?"

"Yes, they raised me after my parents died."

"And they're farmers?"

"Not so much anymore. But they still have the home place. It's not far outside of Green Bay."

"Then you better not spread it around that you're from D. C. They might remember the last time the Redskins beat the Packers."

"I think that was twenty years ago."

"Cheeseheads have long memories."

"Thanks for the warning. See you next year. Gotta' go!" Philip headed for the door. "Happy new year!"

"Right back at'cha! Have a safe trip, boss"

The door swung closed behind Phillip, and in less than a minute frost had obscured the four letter acronym stenciled on the glass; SETI: government-speak for Search for Extraterrestrial Intelligence.

New Year's Day 7:00 am.

Phillip steered the big SUV into the barely visible gap in the six to eight-foot drifts of snow that were piled up against the hedges along the front of his aunt and uncle's front yard. He'd been lucky at the airport. He got the last real SUV to be had from any rental agency in the place. It was the real deal; V8, four wheel drive, big tires. Something built for the crap he was dealing with. Not some soccer-mom's wanna' be. Hitting the driveway was a 50/50 shot at best. But he made it. He was glad. Taking out twenty feet of hedge wouldn't be a very good belated Christmas present.

Aunt Marie met him on the front porch, wrapped in one of those blankets with arms that were all the rage fifteen years ago on middle-of-the-night infomercials. Still, she looked far warmer than he felt after the brief but difficult trudge from the SUV to the house. He'd seen many storms like this one in the years between his parent's death on a snowy night like this, when his aunt and uncle had taken him in and the time his surprisingly high IQ brought him a full-ride scholarship to MIT.

Phillip reached around his aunt and made sure the funny blanket was pulled snuggly up under her chin. He had to crouch a little, since he was easily a head taller than she was now, just the opposite of the seemingly million times when he was ten that she saw him off on the school bus on frigid mornings. He didn't mind. He'd have happily carried her through a mile of snow if it were necessary. When they were two feet from the door it swung open and Uncle Phil hurried them in, throwing one arm around his wife and the other around Phillip. He ushered her to a comfortable-looking chair before the big stone fireplace with its roaring fire. Then he clapped Phillip on the back and apologized over and over for being so slow getting the door open.

"Don't worry about it, Uncle Phil, Captain Kirk couldn't have asked for a door to open any quicker. Now let me get to that fire!" Phillip hurried across the room to the fireplace, and dropped to a cross-legged position in front of it on the thick carpet.

Aunt Marie smiled at him beautifully and said, "It's been too long since we've seen you sitting there like that, Phillip, much too long."

His uncle Phil, after whom he'd been named, said, "Give the boy a break, Marie, he just got here. Don't scold."

"I'm not scolding. I just remember him sitting right there just like that when he was little, and I miss it. I'd like to see him sitting there more often."

"I know Marie, I'm just picking." Then he asked, "Phillip, you want me to pull you a chair in from the other room?"

Phillip said, "No. I'm fine Uncle Phil."

Then he said to his aunt, "I miss this too, Aunt Marie."

"Good enough." His uncle Phil said in his matter-of-fact we've got that taken care of way. "Well, I know the coffee's hot. As soon as you two have got the chill off we'll see about some breakfast." Then he scowled at his wife; something that happened no more often than yearly at the most. "What in the heck where you doing out there in this blizzard in nothing but that goofy blanket thing? What were you thinking?"

Phillip said, "I was wondering about that myself. That didn't seem really smart."

"I'm fine," Phillip's aunt replied. "I was anxious to see our nephew. And

I still had my pajamas on and I pulled my tall boots on. I've been a farm girl my whole life, you know. I've been out in the snow before."

"Yes, dear, I know that," her husband said. "But you're not a kid feeding chickens on your parents' farm any more. All your life up till today is longer than it used to be, and I don't want all your life starting tomorrow to be cut short by a bout of pneumonia brought on by a bought of foolishness this morning."

"Okay, she answered. "Now, you get into the kitchen and pour us coffee and I'll fix us some bacon and eggs."

A little later, with full stomachs and full coffee cups in hand the three of them again sat before the fire. This time Phillip had accepted his uncle's offer of a chair. They caught up on what was happening with far-flung family. Phillip was completely sincere when he told them he was sorry work hadn't allowed him to come for Christmas. Government budget cutbacks meant that scientists were often called on to pick up slack for different departments on short notice. His uncle Phil asked what a specialist in looking for space men could do for other branches of the government. Look for intelligent life in Congress maybe?

Phillip said, "I'm a physicist. I don't sit at a telescope. We have specialists to do that. Then the really brilliant ones in government decide whether the paper should come off the top or bottom of the roll.

Finally talk came around to the sample. Uncle Phil asked, "Well son, did you get a look at that cloth?"

Phillip hesitated before answering.

"What's up boy? It is cloth, isn't it? It felt kind of funny."

"Hold on a second, I forgot." Phillip went to his coat on a peg by the door and retrieved an envelope from an inner pocket. He settled back in his chair and unfolded a long sheet of paper from the envelope. "Well", he began. "It was pretty amazing. The note you sent with the scrap of…" Phillip paused as if not exactly how to proceed.

"Cloth?" His uncle prompted.

Phillip looked again at the paper. "Well, it was woven."

"So it is fabric?" his aunt asked.

"It appears so. But it's unlike anything I've ever seen before."

"How so?" his uncle asked.

Again Phillip referred to the printout. "Well when you look at it it's clearly red. But when we tried to examine it more thoroughly, especially in low light conditions it altered and became very different, very indistinct, almost as if intended to be unseen. It's also as tough as nails. It's hard to study something like that, because there are some tests you can only run on something by destroying a piece of it. But I'd guess it's really old. There are a few visible scuffs on it and what look and smell very slightly like soot stains."

Phillip's aunt and uncle shared a glance that he missed.

"Where did you find it?" Phillip asked his uncle.

"It was hanging on the corner of the chimney Christmas morning. I knocked it down with an old fishing rod, and stuck it in the mail next-day-air to you the following morning.”

“Are you serious?”

His uncle narrowed his eyes. “Serious as a car crash.”

“I believe you.”

The storm had abated, and the late morning sun shone brightly through the east-facing living room windows. Aunt Marie’s homemade coco was a much better suited drink for that kind of day than the morning’s overindulgence in coffee for the sake of warmth had been.

The afternoon was spent with nothing going on but the beginning of a melt. And Phillip was thoroughly enjoying the lazy company of family while waiting for a call that the airport was reopened.

As evening was coming on early, the way mid-winter evenings do, Phillip’s phone rang in his pocket, startling him from a light doze, causing him to let out a small yelp.

His aunt called from the kitchen, “You okay, Hon?”

“Yeah, Aunt Marie, it was just my phone.”

“It’s not the airport already, is it?” She sounded concerned and somewhat displeased that they might lose him already.

Phillip glanced at his caller ID. “Nope, it’s my assistant Wendy, checking in with me.” He took the call

“Tell her we said hello.” His aunt instructed.

"Will do Aunt Marie."

Then to Wendy, Phillip asked, "Did the high flyers get back to you yet?"

"Yes."

"And?"

"Their results and conclusions are the same as ours. What should I do boss?"

"Phillip could barely speak, his voice trying to tremble with excitement. "Go ahead; set it up; as soon as you can. You know the drill. Keep me posted. I'll let you know when I can get a flight back. And my aunt and uncle say hi. Good work. Thanks Wendy. See you soon."

"Be safe boss, bye."

A little while later his uncle built up the fire before they had dinner. Then as they together cleared the table, talk again turned to the strange piece of cloth that wasn't cloth. "So, where is that thing now boy, did you bring it with you?"

"No, I asked another lab to look at it. They concurred with our findings."

"What lab was that?" his uncle asked curiously.

"NASA."

"NASA! Why the rocket jockeys?"

Feeling like he was being scolded, Phillip said, "Don't worry; I'll make sure you get it back. You found it. It's yours. You two will get credit for the discovery."

Phillip's Aunt Marie started crying, quietly at first, but quickly growing in volume, then quickly turning to gales of laughter. She looked at Phillip and said, "Honey you've got your mother's eyes." Then as if rehearsed, his Uncle Phil added, "And your father's knack for jumping to silly conclusions.

January1 8:00 pm.

"I wish you'd perk up," Aunt Marie said, pulling her odd blanket thing around her. They were again huddled around the fireplace, because it seemed like the place to be on a cold winter evening. The oil furnace rumbled, blowing warm air that kept the farmhouse perfectly comfortable, but the fireplace just felt right.

"I made you cry," Phillip said.

"But you also made her laugh harder than I've heard her laugh in years," his uncle said. A big smile spread across his face at the recent memory.

"We're going to hate to see you leave so soon. You just got here."

""I know. But the airline called. The airport's open. I can get a flight out at midnight. And Wendy called. She's got a press conference arranged for tomorrow at five pm."

His aunt shook her head. "Midnight, that's terrible. Just the sound of it scares me."

His uncle said, "Press conference, huh?" All because of the piece of cloth I found stuck to my chimney. You and the boys from NASA think you got it all figured out. That rag must have come from outer space, right?"

Phillip nodded. "It's the only possibility. Stop and think about it. All the incredible properties that sample presented could only have been created by a civilization far more advanced than ours. Finally, it's proof positive." Phillip leaned forward as he spoke. It's a solution to one of the oldest mysteries of the ages."

His uncle smiled sagely and said, "I believe you're trying to convince yourself as much as me."

"What do you mean?"

"What's your I.Q?" Phillip's Aunt asked out of nowhere.

Phillip looked embarrassed.

"Come on boy, spit it out," his uncle said. We know the number is higher than my average weekly salary was for most of my adult life." He laughed as he said it, so Phillip knew he wasn't being made fun of. "I also recall coming home once when you were twelve and finding a half inch of water on the bathroom floor because you weren't sure whether the shower curtain goes inside or outside the tub."

"I don't remember that." Phillip's aunt said.

"I had the boy's back. The bathroom floor got an extra mopping that week. And you didn't even notice. "

He said to Phillip," Son, my point is, sometimes really intelligent people are so busy being intelligent that they don't take time to be smart. No offense meant."

"None taken, but what do you mean?"

"I think you're missing the forest for not believing in the trees."

"I don't get it."

"Where's your printout? Let's take another look.

Phillip got the paper from his coat and started reading aloud. "Woven material; red in color to the naked eye, but the color shifts dramatically and becomes vague and hard to discern, nearly invisible, when studied closely, especially in low light."

"Like at night," his uncle said.

Phillip read on, "Age impossible to pinpoint, but extremely old, also very durable, indeed to the point of being nearly indestructible. The very few visible signs of wear are marked by multiple overlapping stains that appear to be wood soot residue, also very old", Phillip continued.

 Phillip's uncle said, "Red, except in low light, like when it's dark out, almost like somebody doesn't want to be seen." And it's really old and really tough. It's been around a very long time and seen some tough use, but it's hardly scuffed at all. And then there's the soot on it, like chimney soot. And I found it stuck to my chimney on Christmas morning. Phillip, those are what we in the detective business call clues."

 Phillip's aunt snickered behind her hand like a kid with a secret.

Phillip looked at her and asked, "Okay, what's so funny?"

His aunt looked at him and said, "Think with your heart instead of your head Phillip."

Uncle Phil said, "Phillip, you're right, you do have proof positive. You have solved one of the oldest mysteries of the ages. Now you just need to think hard and decide if it's a mystery that really should be solved. Don't you think there are some mysteries that we need?"

After a moment, Philip asked his uncle, "Did Santa bring you what you wanted this year, Uncle Phil?"

The man walked to his wife's side and placed his hand on her shoulder before answering. "Son, I'm seventy-nine, and your aunt's seventy-six. We've been together fifty-seven years. We were still able to take each-other's hands on Christmas morning and when we did they were both still warm. There wasn't anything else Santa needed to bring us."

At nine o'clock Phillip's aunt and uncle said their goodbyes and went to bed. He stayed up and did some thinking, then made a couple calls and watched an old Christmas movie on TV. He was surprised to catch it. Usually by New Year's Day the networks had mothballed them for another year. He remembered that 'Santa Claus Is Coming to Town' was always his favorite when he was little.

Before he sacked down for the night he wrote his aunt and uncle a note which he left on the kitchen counter where they'd see it in the morning. He didn't want to startle them too much when they found he was still there. His flight was rescheduled and he was spending a few more days in Green Bay visiting. The press conference was canceled. He'd decided some mysteries really were better left unsolved. Even with proof positive.

The end

The Legend of The Last Snowflake

Nearly everyone is familiar with the phrase 'The straw that broke the camel's back.'

Those who aren't familiar with it are the lucky ones. Sometimes people throw their arms in the air and shout, "That's the last straw." And then they give up.

There is a very old legend, said to be of Norse origin, passed down from Norwegian father to son from generation to generation, for how many centuries no one truly knows.

The legend goes:

It was the night of St. Nicholas' first Christmas Eve flight. Santa was still a young man then and was very anxious, as flying a sleigh around the world is a big job, and one that he had never done before. But it was something he knew was very important, and he didn't want to let anybody down. He had chosen the reindeer that he felt had the most magic, but they too were young and hadn't flown before, so they were also nervous.

When the time came for Santa to leave on his trip, the sleigh was all loaded, the reindeer were hitched up and the elves were gathered around to wave goodbye. But when Santa flicked the reins and shouted "Now dash away! dash away! dash away all!" the reindeer pulled as hard as they could, but the sleigh wouldn't move an inch. Santa flicked the reins and again shouted his magic chant, and the elves pushed, but the sleigh wouldn't budge. Then Santa looked around and thought hard and saw what the problem was. There wasn't enough snow for the sleigh to glide on. It had been snowing all day, but it still was not enough for the big heavy sleigh, all loaded down with presents to move forward.

Everybody knows that reindeer, even magic reindeer, can't get a sleigh off the ground without a running start.

But they didn't give up. The reindeer pulled even harder. They pawed at the snow, kicking it back under the sleigh's runners. The elves stood in front of the sleigh, waving their arms toward it, creating a breeze to blow the falling snowflakes in the direction of the sleigh. Slowly the snow began building up beneath the big runners and all at once the last snowflake came down. It didn't seem special, but it was. The sleigh gave a big unexpected lurch *and away they all flew like the down of a thistle.*

And the elves all threw their arms in the air and shouted, "That's the last snowflake!" Then they cheered.

Like many legends, especially the very old ones, there is a lesson here:

There wasn't anything special about that last snowflake except it happened to be the very one that was needed to move Santa's sleigh.

There might not be anything special about the pint of blood you donate, except to the person whose life it saves.

There might not be anything special about the pair of socks you give, except to the person whose feet are freezing.

There might not be anything special about your name when you sign it on the bottom of a birthday card, except to the shut-in it goes to.

Don't be surprised if nobody throws their arms in the air and shouts, "That's the last snowflake!"

It might be that nobody knows those things were special. You might not know it yourself. But that's okay;

Those old Norwegians were pretty smart.

The end

SOMETHING SPECIAL

"Jeremiah, did I hear you go out last night after dark?"

"Yes Mother. I took the donkey cart out."

"Why in the world would you do that? Your father will be very upset with you when he finds out."

"No Mother, Father already knows. It was he who told me to go. Soon after sundown the innkeeper from the edge of the city came pounding at the door."

"Why?"

"He seemed very excited. He practically begged Father to deliver a cart of our cleanest hay to the stable behind his inn. He said he had a feeling something very special was going to happen last night. He didn't know what, but he said he wanted to be prepared. He seemed so certain that father had me load the cart full of fresh-cut hay and lead it to his inn. And Mother, I felt it too; something special."

"Still, sending you out into the night, in the cold and the dark; especially with so many strangers coming into the city to be taxed might have been dangerous."

"I was all right Mother. I was walking quickly, leading the donkey, so I wasn't cold. And it wasn't really so dark. There was a very bright star overhead."

"So? Something special? I suppose we'll never know."

"We don't know that Mother.   Who knows? Maybe something special <u>did</u> happen. Maybe something so special happened that the whole world will know about it.

The end

A NEW YEAR'S STORY

The Rocket Man's Luminary

Of course his name wasn't really the rocket man, though that's what he'll always be to me, and also to most of the other townspeople who knew him and remember him in the small burg where I grew up. I've discovered that not a lot of people ever get to meet a truly special person, and fewer yet get to not only meet a truly special person, but really learn what it is that makes that person special. I don't mean what acne cream an eighty-four pound model uses to make her the most special thing in the magazines this week. I mean what it is in a person that sets them apart; what makes them tick, and leaves no doubt that what they think matters. And that what they do will matter. The Rocket Man was one of those people. When he spoke, it was like that old investment company commercial where everybody around goes silent and cups a hand behind an ear to listen. Because there was no doubt that whatever came out of his mouth was, in a word, smart.

Before I tell about him, perhaps I should tell just a little bit about myself.

I made my landing on this third stone from the sun, as Jimi Hendrix called it, on September eighteenth of 1953, when dinosaurs ruled the earth.

That makes me sixty four years of age as I put this on paper. And it's getting close to time to say goodbye to another December, which is what brought memories of the Rocket Man's luminary to mind again as it always does toward the end of year.

To begin, the Rocket Man's actual name was Jonas Hughes. He was an extremely distinguished looking black man with steel-gray hair. I first met him when I was in grade school (what is now called elementary). I have no clue why that is. I'm sure there's some important bureaucratic reason. Mister Hughes (aka the Rocket Man) served in Vietnam with my brother. They were both U S Air Force. Mister Hughes spent most of his hitch mounting Sidewinder missiles under the wings of F4 Phantom fighters after he was shot down in the rear seat of one very early on and got his purple heart. All that time mounting under-wing rockets earned him the Rocket Man nick-name, and he brought it home with him, along with a bad shoulder from the shock of being ejected from a falling jet. Along the way he got to offering some very intelligent suggestions for improvements to the missiles, that when applied, improved their accuracy and kill rate by over ten percent. Needless to say, my brother had a great deal of respect for the Rocket Man, as did most of the people in my home town, with the exception of the town's few redneck bigots who were still living in the past, though by the late sixties their kind was on the leading edge of a dying breed that sadly refuses to become extinct even now. But even most of them shut up when it came out that the Rocket Man had also served in The U.S. Army in Korea and had also earned a purple heart there near the end of what our government insisted on calling a conflict, not a war. From there he brought home a limp to go with his bad shoulder.

As I have stated, I met the Rocket Man when I was in elementary school, but the story of his luminary began a lot of years later in 1980.

It turned out that Mister Hughes was as smart as he was patriotic.

After his second honorary discharge from his second war Mister Hughes invested the fairly large amount of money he'd saved while on the government payroll during one war and one "conflict" and invested it wisely. Within a dozen years he was the wealthiest man in our town and for quite a few miles around.

Well, like a lot of small towns, ours had benefited financially from the cold war. We sat right on the east coast and a big chunk of our local economy revolved around the Army Depot outside of town. It really amounted to nothing more than a big parking lot, a barracks with a small yard and garden in front of the officer's quarter, and a parade ground. It was mostly all olive-drab and spotless asphalt; the best American tax dollars could provide. The local paint store kept a big stock of the olive-drab, and the area's biggest asphalt contractor was under priority contract.

It was all behind twelve-foot chain-link fence, topped with coiled razor-wire. The regional Long-Fence Man sent his Son to Dartmouth on that contract. A one-ring circus could have pitched their tent inside of it. But the most I ever saw through that fence was eighteen jeeps and a dozen troop transports. As military bases went it wasn't much. I understand no more than a dozen of the thirty bunks in the barracks were ever slept in at the same time. Still, the men who were stationed there did frequently visit the town's stores, restaurants, and one tavern when off duty. To their credit, I never heard of them causing one fight in the tavern.

At his peak, Noland Ryan could have thrown a baseball from the East end of the parade ground into the Atlantic Ocean. That's the end that had the forty-foot tall flag pole that becomes so important later in my story.

The Mess, (kitchen to the non-military familiar) was kept stocked and ready, as was the Infirmary (hospital) and since many of those items had limited shelf lives they were bought locally. The town's hardware and nursery stores got a spring boost from plant and mulch sales as the Privates stuck with after-winter clean up detail got to work. Also a few mowers, shovels, rakes, and post hole diggers. And gallons and gallons of insecticides, pesticides, grass seed and the like bought in bulk. Those were before the days of the mega home centers as big as the base. Those were also the days before the U.S. Government decided that dozens of small military bases were no longer cost effective and should be closed. You may at this point correctly deduce before I go any further that our base was one of those.

It hurt the town. It hurt the town bad. How bad my town was hurt compared to other towns that went through the same experience I can't say. I didn't live in those towns. I lived here. Also writing it all down for our little newspaper was my job, along with the obituaries, bake sales and human interest stories; meaning, of course, the stories that were of interest to the humans in our town. And, as it turned out some humans who were not even close to our town. For that, I have to take credit, if I do say so myself. I got a summer job at the local paper sweeping up the press room between my freshman and sophomore years in school, stayed on in the evenings between school years. I then became a pressman, and eventually when I graduated from school I moved upstairs behind a typewriter, then a computer. That's how I learned Mister Hughes' story.

As I mentioned before, the Rocket Man was a very wise investor, so when Uncle Sam decided to put a For-Sale sign on the base he no longer deemed essential, the first and only bidder was the Rocket Man. Mister Hughes immediately donated the barracks building to the local Methodist Church, on the condition that it be used as a homeless shelter. The base also had a basketball court and tennis court for use by the troops stationed there. They were nothing fancy, but equal to or better than those at the local park. They were immediately opened for public use during daylight hours. In no time they were swarming with town kids and teenagers whose parents were thrilled to now know where they were spending their time.

Soon after that he rented a small backhoe called a Bobcat and had it delivered to the base. Word spread like wild fire and the next morning a crowd of locals were lined up along the chain-link fence rubber-necking like aliens had landed. I know because I was one of them. We weren't disappointed. There were no aliens, but there was entertainment. At least for an entertainment deprived town like ours.

One thing must be said for Mister Hughes; aka the Rocket Man. His plan was well thought out, and well prepared for. At six a.m. Mister Hughes drove up in his blue Dodge pickup, unlocked the gate, and pulled onto the parade ground like he owned the place,(which he did). He stopped his truck eight or ten feet from the base of the flag pole and climbed out.

After nodding politely at the crowd of people gawking rudely at him like a bug in a jar, the Rocket Man fired up the engine of the Bobcat and drove it to a spot about halfway from the big flagpole to the East fence. From where he stopped the machine he no doubt had a beautiful early-morning view of the Atlantic broken up into a thousand little diamond-shaped fragments.

Then, moving quickly and efficiently, qualities reflecting on a lifetime of military training, he strapped on a tool belt and unloaded two things from his truck; a large acetylene torch mounted on a two-wheeled cart, and an extension ladder. He rolled the torch to the base of the flagpole then turned his attention to the ladder. Pulling the rope on the ladder, he slid it smoothly and silently up to the length he wanted and leaned it against the flagpole. I have a feeling that no mechanical device belonging to Mister Hughes ever made a squeak or rattle.

Next he walked to the back of the Bobcat and pulled a coil of steel cable from under the seat. One end of the cable he secured to the bolt that served as a towing point on rear of the small machine, and then placed the coil neatly on the asphalt. Then he started the Bobcat's engine and let it idle.

You must realize that as all this was happening, the crowd of rubberneckers gathered outside the fence was growing larger. I recall being amazed that Mister Hughes just went about his business with no more concern than if a crowd was gathered to watch him wash his car, or mow his grass; which, of course would be ridiculous. While everybody else just watched, I watched and, as I was by then a reporter, scribbled notes as fast as I was able. I went through three Bic pens that day, and suffered what must be the most miserable case of writer's cramp in human history. It was to Mister Hughes' credit that he had no issue with us staring through the fence at him. I believe I already mentioned some of his actions since purchasing the defunct base that showed his concern for others more than himself. Perhaps he felt that a town that had recently suffered the financial setback that the base's closing had brought could use the entertainment he was providing. Had he wished to get rid of us, he'd have been within his rights. He owned not only what was inside the fence, but what was around it for a hundred yards in every direction.

I didn't find out till later that what he was doing simply meant more to him than what any of those crowded around the fence might think.

He stopped and looked the flagpole over from bottom to top, like a man checking out a very tall tree. He then sparked the big torch alight. It came to life with a loud pop like a champagne cork amplified a hundred times. Some of the people oohed and aahed like they were watching fireworks. With a quick flip of his wrist he pulled a couple loops of hose from the cart and went to the base of the pole. He began working the blue-white flame over the metal about two feet above the asphalt. The military-gray paint blistered and peeled back immediately, the air reeking with the smell. In moments the steel beneath was glowing red. He walked around the pole, being cautious to keep the torch hose away from the hot metal. He worked the flame up and down, all the way around. When he'd made a full circle, the pole was glowing red from about two to four feet above the ground.

Then things really became interesting. He shut the torch off and dropped the nozzle on the ground. For the first time since he'd driven through the gate he seemed to be rushing. He hurried to the coil of cable lying on the asphalt at the back of the Bobcat. There was the kind of spring clip they call a carabiner attached to the opposite end of the cable from that he'd hooked to the idling machine. He quickly clipped it to his tool belt. Then with a grace and agility belying his age, he went to the ladder and began climbing.

Within seconds, he was at the top of the ladder; a point that appeared to be about half way to the top of the pole, or roughly two stories above the asphalt. Reaching behind him, he unclipped the carabiner from the tool belt and fastened it to a stout looking metal bracket clamped to the pole that I personally hadn't noticed before. Whether anybody else had, I can't say. Then he came back down with a speed that would have landed me in the back of an ambulance, though he was nearly three times my age.

He got in the seat of the Bobcat, and looking over his shoulder, began driving slowly toward the Atlantic Ocean.

As the crowd watched, astounded, the flagpole gradually began to tilt. It bent at the point he'd heated with the torch like there was a hinge there. The little backhoe crept forward, its engine barely above an idle. It was hardly moving, and in a matter of seconds it came to a halt. The Rocket Man looked over his shoulder once more and then killed the engine.

He climbed down and went to the back of the machine and unhooked the cable. He stepped back to inspect his handiwork. Then he wiped his hands on his pants, nodded to the crowd of onlookers and walked to his truck. Behind him the forty foot tall flagpole was now tilted at an angle that to my untrained eye looked to be about twenty-five or thirty degrees. It was like a long steel finger pointed directly into the red morning sun, still on the rise over the ocean, surrounded by the kind of brilliant blue sky particular to Atlantic mornings; with only the slightest wisps of white clouds that looked like cotton hanging just above the horizon . Though I still had no clue what it was all about; or why he had done what he had done, I desperately wished I had a camera. It would have made an amazing picture for the front page of the paper.

I can't speak for anybody else, of course, as I only know how I was feeling at that moment. But speaking for myself; I had an almost irrepressible urge to cheer as Mister Hughes unlocked the gate, drove through, and stopped to lock it behind him. I know how ridiculous that must sound to anyone else. It sounds ridiculous to me as I write it down. But by then I had come to realize that he was one of those rare truly special people I've previously mentioned. So bending a flagpole obviously seemed like a special thing; because special people do special things. It made perfect sense; though it made no sense at all.

But, I was the only one who seemed to view what we had seen as anything of importance, as anything more than a brief distraction. In no time the crowd of onlookers who'd been lined up elbow to elbow like kids watching a ballgame grew tired of muttering amongst themselves and meandered off to their cars and went home. I stood there for more than an hour; staring at the flagpole and wondering how much planning had gone into what we had watched; if any had at all, beyond renting the little backhoe. After all, a man who gave the U. S. military tips on how to improve their weaponry probably didn't have to devote a lot of brain power to tilting a flagpole toward the ocean. He could probably have worked it out over breakfast or maybe while shaving one morning.

I would be setting a new world record for understatement to say I was surprised to receive a phone call from the Rocket Man the day after the morning of the flagpole bending. It hadn't taken long for it to take on special event status in my mind; "The flagpole bending." Like "The Christmas tree lighting" or "The lunar eclipse" or something of the sort.

When I answered the phone, of course, he didn't introduce himself as the rocket man. He simply said it was Jonas Hughes and asked if I would mind stopping by his house the next morning around eight. He then proceeded to give me his address, though I'd known where he lived most of my life. I assured him I'd be there and spent the rest of the day wondering what in the world he could want of me and mentally beating myself up for not just asking when I had the chance. I had simply been taken by surprise.

Mister Hughes cleared up the mystery quickly and succinctly over coffee on his patio the next morning. As it turned out, he knew who I was, too; a fact that made me practically glow with pride, though I shouldn't have been surprised. My brother had introduced me to him back when I was a kid, and he seemed like a very detail-oriented individual. Not the sort of man who would let a name slip his mind. Especially not the name of the brother of a man with whom he'd served.

He had noticed me standing outside the fence the previous day, scribbling frantically in my note pad while seemingly the whole population of our town had nothing else to do, and so had decided to congregate around the former military base and watch him go about his business. Business that was really nobody's but his.

He either had already known I worked for the paper or had made the effort to find out, and explained that the reason for his call was to ask if I might be interested in hearing what was his reason for bending the flagpole. I have to admit here that at that point I had to cross my legs to hold in a sudden excitement-induced stream of urine. For my little town's newspaper this was about as interesting as human interest could possibly get. Had I known then what I know now, my pants would have been soaked. But, I'm getting ahead of myself.

We sipped coffee on his patio. In a while he asked how I liked my eggs, to which I answered over easy. He excused himself to the kitchen and in just a few short moments returned one-handing a wooden tray loaded with two plates filled with omelets that smelled wonderful and set my stomach to growling; reminding me that my adjusted morning schedule hadn't allowed for breakfast. In his other hand he carried the carafe from his Mister-Coffee. I relieved him of that part of his burden so he could set the tray down. As he did so, I topped off our cups.

After we ate we exchanged pleasantries for a while, and then he said that seeing me scribbling in my note pad made it clear that I was more than a little bit interested in his flagpole project. And he thought that whether I found his story newsworthy or not, he figured his explaining it might satisfy my curiosity as well as give him a chance to get some things off of his chest. That statement cranked my curiosity up from a nine to a ten. If it had been a Spinal Tap amp it would have definitely nailed eleven. Before he started I asked if he would be okay with my writing up what he told me for the paper; after he proofed it, of course. I hadn't, of course, heard a word of what he was about to share but had a bone-deep feeling it was something that was too important to be shared with only me. He sighed deeply, then nodded and began to talk. This is what he said, as closely and accurately as I was able to keep up with writing it down;

"As you know I was in two wars, in two branches of the service. The second time was in Viet Nam where I served with your brother."

Here I remember nodding. I tried not to say anything unless he asked me a question, as I didn't want to derail his train of thought. He had the look in his eyes of a man whose mind was looking backwards. How far back I didn't know. I concentrated on being ready when he was ready to talk about the present again. He sipped his cold coffee

"Nam was like Korea in a lot of ways. Too damn many ways. Nobody won, but we sure did lose.

Just like in Korea, young men; hell boys, lost their innocence way too early. Too many people; men *and* women lost their faith and belief in what human beings are, or should be. Too many men, who went over there caring about life, lost that ability. When I saw men coming back from flights laughing about seeing burning people running from the villages in flames from the napalm I felt the loss in the whole human race." Here his voice hitched and his eyes were wet.

"Then, of course, there was the physical loss. Just like in Korea, ruined limbs were removed and tossed away by the hundreds, or thousands. So some lost the ability to walk, others to tie their own shoes, or wipe their own ass." He paused. For the first time anger had begun to creep into his voice, slight at first, but deepening. That pause was imperative. He knew it and I knew it. It prevented something inside him from boiling over. Something that had been simmering for a long time. Then he said, "A lot of limbs lost, and a lot of lives lost. Two wars that nobody won, but we definitely lost. And <u>that's</u> why I bent that flagpole." He fell silent. I put a period in my note pad. I didn't see till later that I had pressed it three pages deep. I waited

"Do you know what a luminary is?" I nodded.

"Well, just like people light candles in bags at memorials to remember people they've lost to senseless killers like cancer and heart disease, I've got a luminary in mind to remember all the losses in two senseless wars." Then he stood and said, "Walk to the garage with me."

His garage was large, with three roll-up aluminum doors. His pick-up sat in one end. A work bench lined the back wall. What was both confusing and amazing sat on a row of planks across a pair of sawhorses in the center bay of the garage. It was what appeared to be a metal sphere about a dozen feet in diameter. He walked to it, nodding for me to follow. When we were close enough for him to touch it, he explained; speaking like a science teacher talking to his class.

"This is all made of aluminum sheets I bent over an old truck tire with a rubber mallet, and tacked welded together."

"But, what is it," I asked.

"My luminary." He pointed out a seam up one side of the sphere and a row of hinges on the opposite side. Then he bent down and indicated four round openings on the underside. "Those are exhaust ports. Inside of this big metal ball are four of the same rocket engines I sent out to kill men in Nam. All purchased military surplus, bought and paid for. This ball will swing open on those hinges and wrap around that bent flagpole. At midnight on New Year's Eve I intend to fire those engines and I will finally launch a fitting luminary to all those losses. The flagpole will guide it out over the ocean like the metal rods kids use to launch their model rockets. That way it will be out where nobody can have a problem with it, if anybody cares about it at all."

"But why a ball, and why New Year's Eve?" I asked.

"When the world's oldest teenager's ball drops, mine will go up. A more positive message, I think; if anybody else notices, that is." I'll point out here that Dick Clark was still doing the New Year's Eve thing in New York back then. "But, even if nobody else does, he continued, I'll know what it means." I recall the last was said quietly, but with a great deal of feeling.

"Mister Hughes", I said when I could speak again, "With your permission, I'd like to do my best to make sure people notice." He shook my hand and I left feeling very honored.

I wrote his story that evening and submitted it to the editor of the paper the following morning. My position on our small-town rag made Jimmy Olson look big-time, but he ran it in the evening edition, and again the following morning.

At that time our town had a monstrous population of just over twelve thousand, three hundred. Probably three quarters of those homes had home delivery and there were two dozen orange boxes scattered over the six blocks of downtown. A few were mailed out of town to people who had moved away. I honestly didn't have a lot of hope of the story being noticed. Though rumors always spread faster than flu spreads in winter, worthwhile news tended to die like roses in winter.

But some people noticed. Our town had a lot of veterans; also a lot of people who respected veterans. When my brother read the story, he cried. But sadly there were, in the early seventies, still a lot of racist bigots. Among that crowd the word uppity was commonly used to describe Mister Hughes, and it wasn't surprising to hear the N word thrown around. There wasn't any internet then, but there was the wire service. My story got picked up and run by some of the big papers.

That was one of those good news/ bad news things. I'll do the bad news first; I didn't win a Pulitzer. Also one of the racist bigots who read my story happened to be the Fire Marshal of our county. He also happened to be one of those who gets a small amount of authority and acts like he's suddenly ruler of this planet and all those in near orbits. To prove it he went clear to the Governor to stop the Rocket Man from launching his luminary on grounds of fire danger. It was a ridiculous claim. Directly beyond the former base's boundary fence a rock wall fell away to the ocean. That was why the site was originally chosen for the base during the cold war; all the harder for Communists to climb up. So there was nothing out there to burn. But the father of the Fire Marshal's wife had been a big donor to the Governor's election campaign. So he got to show how important he was.

Then for the good news; I got a call at my desk that I thought must be a joke when they first told me who it was. It was someone else who had read my story and found it interesting. Someone who'd been a fighter pilot in Korea, and had more than a small amount of interest in rockets. He asked me if I thought Mister Hughes would be willing to send him a copy of his plans, if he had any. I told him I'd definitely ask and see what I could do. I got the plans and put them in the mail; first class, special delivery, at my own expense.

The good news; no, the <u>very</u> good news; at twelve am January first 1980 the Rocket Man's luminary arched out over the Atlantic. It wasn't a widely known event, but it definitely mattered.

And the interesting part; I imagine the Governor thought it was a joke when his secretary told him who was on the phone, too.

Our town's Rocket Man received the endorsement of the former fighter pilot who I had spoken to and sent the plans to. He was also a rocket man, the one who had once said "That's one small step for man, and one giant leap for mankind."

I imagine the Governor pretty quickly stopped caring about the Fire Marshal <u>and</u> his family.

That's the story of the Rocket Man's Luminary.

-30 –

(that's news-writer speak for the end)

www.ingramcontent.com/pod-product-compliance
Lightning Source LLC
Chambersburg PA
CBHW071945190726